The Editor's Choice

Hannah France

For my wonderful husband.

Thank you for all of your support. I truly could not have done it without you.

Also, my best friend.

Thank you for all the late-night reads and your unwillingness to let me give up on my dreams.

It wasn't supposed to go this way....

Emily was my best friend in the entire world. We met when we were about six, in the same class, and were inseparable ever since. We literally did everything together for years.

That all changed last week.

Now there's no going back and nothing will ever be the same.

Fuck. This.

Chapter One

Jade

"What the fuck," I whisper, staring at the messages on his phone. "What in the actual fuck is this?" I continue, feeling my pulse escalate and heat flush my face. It has to be early morning, judging by the soft light filtering in through the curtained windows.

Dawson stirs and mumbles, but within a few seconds, his breathing evens back out, completely dead to the world.

Dawson. My Dawson. We've been together just over four years now and everything has been incredible. We're the definition of high school sweethearts, or so I thought. We met in middle school and became best friends nearly instantly.

Dawson, Emily, and I became an inseparable trio, continuing our friendship into high school and college.

Though things have been a bit more complicated since we left college, we've maintained our friendship and still get together a couple times a week when our schedules work out.

As a matter of fact, we just saw Emily last night when she was here at our place, hanging out after a night of drinking and karaoke. We had gone out to the bar for a few hours, then crashed here, promising to take her back to her apartment in the morning. She's still here, sleeping in the guest room down the hall.

Scanning over the texts again, I take Dawson's phone and quietly slip out of bed, careful not to risk waking him. I need some space to figure out what the hell is going on. Padding on bare feet, I slide the glass door to the patio open, stepping out into the crisp morning air.

EMILY: Does she really have to know though?

DAWSON: We can't keep having these conversations, Em. She's going to find out eventually.

EMILY: Ughhhhhhh. I guess you're right. It's probably best if we're just honest with her about it

now. I just don't want to lose you guys because of this whole mess…

My stomach churns, threatening to spew all the alcohol from last night at any second. My head spins, making me feel dizzy and disoriented.

There's no way this is happening.

Locking his phone, I place it face down on the table next to me as I watch the sunrise, desperately trying to extinguish the burn in my chest and calm my pulse. Acting insane isn't going to fix anything. I just need some time to figure out what's going on and how to move forward from here.

Nearly tiptoeing, I place the phone back on Dawson's nightstand before heading for the kitchen to start a pot of coffee. While that is brewing, I put a few of the dishes away, clearing the space of any unnecessary clutter.

My mind is whirling with a trillion thoughts as I absentmindedly grab a mug from the cupboard and open the fridge door for the creamer. "Fuck!" I start, nearly jumping out of my skin, hand flying to my chest. My heart is beating erratically against my ribcage from the scare. "I didn't hear you come in."

Emily stands on the other side of the kitchen, rubbing the back of her hand against her eye. She groans before dropping onto one of the bar stools and holding her hand out for a coffee. Withholding the eye roll, I pour her a cup of coffee and hand it over, which earns me a tiny hint of a smile.

Before I open my big fat mouth and say what's on my mind, I place my mug on the counter and head off toward the bedroom. I hadn't planned on starting the day with a shower, but I need space before I explode.

With Dawson still asleep in our bed, I quietly close the bathroom door and turn on the hot water. While waiting for it to warm up, I stare at my own eyes in the mirror, searching for I don't even know what at this point. Hope? Understanding perhaps? Maybe even a hint at what I'm supposed to do going forward.

While I don't have all the answers, it seems pretty obvious that Emily and Dawson have been seeing each other behind my back. Roughly pulling my hand down my face, I turn from the mirror and focus on things I can control for now. Removing my pajamas, I step into the hot water, steam now rolling from the walk-in shower.

This shower is hands down my favorite part of the entire house. We had it custom built when we bought the place. It's all black tile with gold grout with his and hers rainfall shower heads. There is also a handheld sprayer for each side and shelves built into the wall in the middle. There's even a bench made into my side for when I want to relax in here.

I step into the hot water, hands clasped around the back of my neck in a pathetic attempt to ease some of the pressure building there. It's starting to give me a headache and that's the last thing I need right now. I take a huge breath, filling my lungs until they feel as if they will burst, then exhale all at once. With that, the first tear slips down my face, joining the rest of the water drops circling down the drain.

Going through the motions, I finish cleaning myself before I collapse onto the bench, turning the handheld sprayer toward my body so I can keep warm. Pulling my legs up to my chest, I wrap my arms around them, leaning into the wall, and let my world crash down around me. Wave after wave of grief threaten to take me under.

I grieve for my relationship. My friendship. Our future. We've all been intertwined so long I can't even imagine moving forward without either of them now. As I'm trying to pull myself together and gather the courage to leave the shower, I hear the door open and the shuffling of feet.

"Babe?" Dawson mumbles, still half asleep. "You never shower this early. Is everything okay?" Of course he would ask. I always shower at night, close to bedtime.

Clearing my throat, I try to force my voice past my teeth, even though my tongue feels as if it's stuck to the roof of my mouth. "Uh, yeah. Everything is fine. I was just feeling rough from all the drinking last night. Thought a hot shower might help take the edge off," I manage. It sounds weak even to my own ears but I'm hoping he will drop it at that.

Scrubbing my hands down my face, hoping against hope that it's not a red and puffy mess, I take a deep breath in and prepare to face the day. Stretching my legs that are now tingling, I stand and shut off the water. Praying my legs continue to hold me up, I open the shower door and grab a towel for my hair. Once it's up and I've dried my body with another towel, I make my way to the sink to moisturize my body. At this point, my routine is the only thing keeping me even halfway sane.

A half hour later, I'm walking into the gym. Ear buds in place with Bad Omens blaring, I do some quick stretches, eager to get started. This place has become my safe space, where I don't have to talk or be polite. I can work out in silence, allowing my mind the space it needs to find solutions that otherwise allude me.

Starting with a brisk walk on the treadmill to warm up, my mind starts to wander. For the first time all morning, I just let it go wherever it pleases, taking me down a path that has little chance of redemption. The questions start to pour in faster and faster until I feel as if I'm drowning in them.

I want to know everything, but they obviously aren't going to tell me the truth if I confront them. If they were going to be honest, I wouldn't have had to find those messages on my own.

Making my way to the leg press, I glance around the gym, noticing how empty it is for the first time. There are only a few people here today. A petite blond girl and a guy I'm assuming is her boyfriend from the way they're touching and giggling at each other. *Fucking disgusting,* I think, rolling my eyes at them. Then I see him.

I've never seen this guy here before, but we lock eyes right after my eyes return to their normal position from the roller coaster I just sent them on. When we lock eyes, I see that he's smirking. Great. I'm going to guess he saw the eye roll. *That's embarrassing.*

Feeling the heat creep up my neck and into my cheeks, I break the eye contact, trying my best to focus on resetting the weights. Although I fumble a bit, I manage to get set up and slide into the seat, placing my feet on the footplate. Soon enough, the world slips away, replaced by the burning in my thighs and the whirlwind of thoughts. My entire world is crumbling and there's not a damn thing I can do about it.

If there is one thing I hate in this world more than anything else, it's feeling helpless. And I'll be damned if I don't feel utterly and totally helpless to the marrow of my bones today.

After pushing myself to the point my legs are shaking with every step, I decide enough is enough and make my way to the front door and back out into the world. I have no clue where I'm going at this point. I just know I can't go home right now. The gym helped some, but I'm still locked in a hopeless battle with my brain.

Turning left as I leave the gym, I find myself walking aimlessly. I don't know where exactly I'm going, just that I need to get away for a few more hours.

Suddenly, I'm snapped out of my thoughts when I notice my cell phone buzzing in my back pocket. I hadn't thought to check it when I left the gym. Not that anything I found there would change anything at this point anyway.

Filling my lungs to the point of bursting, I slowly exhale before fishing the phone out of my pocket to see who's calling. I don't answer when I see Dawson's name flashing across the screen. Within a few seconds, the call ends and a shit ton of notifications pop up. Seven missed calls. Nineteen texts. Eight Snapchat notifications.

As I slide my phone back into my pocket, I'm hit with an overwhelming sense of numbness. I have no desire to answer either of them right now. Their bullshit excuses are just not what I'm in the mood for. I need time to clear my head before I deal with either of them.

Instead of heading back toward home, I turn the opposite direction and make my way to a place I used to love as a kid.

***

Almost an hour later, I finally plop down on the cliff's edge, overlooking the river. When I was younger, I came here all the time to get away from home and all the drama there. Luckily, very few people know about this place, so I have the entire area to myself right now.

I had considered bringing Dawson here from time to time, but now I'm thankful I never got around to it. Something about it just never felt quite right, so I kept putting it off.

My thoughts are interrupted when my phone starts buzzing yet again. "Dear fucking God, can't you get the hint already?!" I scream into the empty space around me. On a split-second decision, I chuck the phone as hard as I can, watching it drop until I lose sight of it all together. With a sigh of contentment, I lay back against the ground, feeling the pebbles stabbing into my back but welcoming the slight pain.

Throwing one arm up over my face to shield my eyes from the sun, I lay there for what feels like hours, absorbing the heat and allowing all the negativity to slowly ebb out of my bones.

Once the air takes on the hint of a chill, I pull myself into a sitting position and do my best to dust off my back after stretching my exhausted muscles. The sun is starting to set, and I really need to get out of here before it's completely dark and I can't see the path anymore.

Stepping over the bigger rocks, I set my mind to figuring out my next move. Dwelling on what they've done isn't going to help. At least not without some sort of plan.

The sound of a twig snapping pulls me out of my thoughts. I swivel my head toward the sound, squinting against the setting sun. Not seeing anything out of the ordinary, I turn back toward the path and take a few steps before the hair on the back of my neck stands up and I'm consumed by a full body cold chill.

I take off at a dead sprint before my mind can even make a conscious decision. Suddenly I'm absolutely terrified, fight or flight kicking in full force. I don't dare slow down until I make it back to a more populated area with some streetlights.

Gasping for breath, hands on my knees, I look back toward the path. There's nothing there, of course. Rolling my eyes at my own fear, I turn and head toward town so I can finally go home and deal with the damages. Although I would have preferred whatever was in the woods, I'm sure.

Chapter Two

Roman

I truly didn't even mean to follow her, yet here I am, watching over her as she hurls her phone out into the abyss. She really has quite the temper apparently.

When I saw her in the gym, something about her just piqued my interest. I can't quite put my finger on it and it's starting to irritate me if I'm being honest.

She isn't anything special to look at honestly. Jet black hair that falls in soft waves to her mid-back, hazel eyes from what I could see. It's obvious she works out frequently but definitely nothing over the top. Average height. There really isn't anything about her that stands out physically.

Over the last several hours, I've come to the conclusion that it must be her aura. The way she carries herself is unlike anything I've witnessed before. One moment, she seems meek, almost like a timid little mouse. The next, something triggers her anger and there's a darkness that rolls through her body. That moment reminds me of a thunderstorm right before the first lightning strike and the thunder that follows right after. The moment before all hell breaks loose.

Maybe that's what it is. I've always been attracted to the chaos and that radiates off her in waves when she's angry.

What in the world am I getting myself into?

Shaking my head to clear the thoughts, I refocus just in time to see her stretch and rise to her feet before dusting herself off. That stretch has to be the cutest thing I've ever seen. It's like the weight of the world has lifted from her shoulders for just a moment, allowing her to breathe freely again.

As she heads back down the trail, the weight resettles and I feel almost a bit sad. The carefree spirit Jade carried just moments earlier is gone and replaced with the storm clouds again.

What's got you so down, sweet girl? Trouble at home? With friends maybe? Perhaps at work? My mind drifts for a bit as I watch her walk slowly back toward civilization. Before I can even catch myself, I'm wondering who has hurt this poor girl and fantasizing about how their blood would look smeared across my hands.

I'm not supposed to be that guy anymore. I guess old habits die hard though, especially when it's something you enjoyed. I learned at a fairly young age that the world isn't fair by any stretch of the imagination. Sometimes you have to take matters into your own hands and find your own justice. Sometimes you have to be the voice for the people who don't have their own anymore.

Snap.

Fuck.

In the silence, the sound is absolutely deafening. Jade instantly turns toward me, seeking out the source. The sun is to my back so I know it will be impossible for her to see anything, but the possibility of being found out has me on edge.

I really should have been paying more attention to where I was stepping. *Fucking idiot.*

When she can't easily identify the source, she quickly switches from fight to flight, taking off at a dead run back toward safety. Although, for just a split second, I'm sure I saw her shiver, as if she could feel my presence without even knowing who I am or why her body reacted at all. Smirking slightly, I slowly make my way toward home, hoping to put all this behind me and forget about her entirely.

***

Last night was spent tossing and turning. I'm pretty sure I didn't get a full hour of sleep all night. Every time I would doze off, the image of Jade, skin covered in goosebumps, standing on the dusty trail, comes barreling into my dreams. Each time, I wake up sweating, panting for breath.

Around 4am, I finally had enough and climbed out of bed, making my way to the office. If I can't sleep, I might as well get some work done.

Opening my laptop, I stir some creamer into my coffee and open up my emails. I didn't check them last night so there are tons to go through this morning but one in particular catches my eye.

It's a new editing request from an author going by the name of J. Adams. The writer has sent a 152-page manuscript of a romance novel according to the blurb. This would be their debut novel. Normally I refuse this type of work, just because debut authors typically don't listen to what I have to say about their work and it's a gigantic pain in my ass. But something about this one has me reconsidering.

After replying to a couple other emails, scheduling a few pressing meetings, and booking a hotel for my upcoming trip, I settle in and open the manuscript. I wanted to say no, but it keeps pulling at my brain, so here we are.

About six chapters in, I start to realize this book is purely fantasies written out in vulgar detail. This is every sexual desire this author has ever had come to life. And it's hot as fuck. Hopefully this person has a partner with half a brain cell because everything they want is laid out in black and white in this book. All you'd have to do is crack the cover and you would know everything you would ever need to do to satisfy them to their core.

I make it to chapter eight before I have to take a break, deciding to research the author a bit. Maybe that would give me a little better idea on the writing style and best way to approach them with my professional opinions. The book is fantastic so far. With a little tweak here and there, I sincerely feel it could be a bestseller. That's a subject I try to approach gently though. Inflating an author's ego is not something that typically goes well at this stage of writing. They get the big head and then stop listening, causing the book to be mediocre at best once it hits print.

A quick Google search doesn't yield anything valuable. It's a common name, which I assume is probably the entire point. Facebook does a little better but still nothing completely solid. It narrows it down quite a bit though, making the Instagram search quick and to the point. Got it. And I'll be damned.

My little thunderstorm.

Her name pops up instantly, showcasing a picture of her and some guy, who I'm assuming is her boyfriend. They're both smiling and happy, enjoying a beach vacation somewhere. My stomach flips, so I focus on scrolling through the page, trying to find anything about this book.

Seven weeks ago, she posted just the title. Bingo.

With my hunch confirmed, I scroll a little farther into her social media, trying to find any tidbit about her I can manage. I'm oddly curious about who she is as a person, not just an author. I want to know what makes her tick. That helps with the editing process, I reason with myself.

There are pictures of her dog, a fuzzy Australian Shepherd with the bluest eyes. I find a few snaps of food here and there. A couple pictures with the guy in her profile picture, though I can't for the life of me figure out what she sees in that guy. From what I've seen, he's the cookie cutter, all-American guy. Blond, green eyes, athletic, high school jock type guy. I'd wager he's just as boring in bed as he is in conversation. Surface level at best.

Whatever. Enough of that, I think, trying to clear away those thoughts. I really need to refocus on reading her manuscript and decide whether it's even worth an edit or not. That is my job, after all.

Another ten minutes of rereading the first paragraph of the second chapter and still not managing to comprehend a single word, I lean back away from the desk and scrub my hands through my hair and then down my face, frustrated to my core. All I can think about is her face. I knew better than to look up her social media, but I had to know for sure that I was right and it was her.

Dear J. Adams,

I received your manuscript and would love to review and edit it. However, this is going to require an in-person meeting so I can get to know you and your style.

This is not my normal requirement, but I am having trouble settling into your story and feel this would help the process along.

Let's grab dinner one night this week to discuss this further. Let me know what works best for you, and I'll accommodate.

-Roman Grato

I hit send and close my laptop before I can remind myself that I'm a damn idiot and change my mind. I've never met a client in person, but there's just something about this girl. I have to get close to her, and if I need to use my career to do that, then so be it.

Chapter Three

Jade

After taking the long way home, I find myself seated at the kitchen table, thinking back on all the memories in this house.

The first time we opened the door, this place just felt like home. Moving all our things in, getting drunk, and laughing until 4am. The insane fight we had over what color to paint the accent wall in the living room. We watched tv on the floor for a week while waiting for our new couch to be delivered. None of that even matters now, but the memories bring tears to my eyes.

All the plans we made were erased with a few careless messages and who knows what else. I don't even want the details of whatever was going on between them. I just want this entire thing to be over so I can move on and forget they ever existed to begin with.

As I slide the gorgeous engagement ring off my finger and place it on the table, I hear the front door unlock and take a deep, steadying breath.

This is going to hurt like fuck.

Except when the door opens, all I can hear is giggling. Carefree laughter fills the house as Emily and Dawson step into the foyer, completely unaware that I'm in the next room. Knowing that neither of them could give a fuck less about my whereabouts fuels a rage inside me that I've never felt before.

The fire in my chest must be visible in my eyes because they both come to a dead stop as soon as they round the corner to the kitchen, eyes landing on me.

"Jade," Emily gasps. "I wasn't expecting you to be here. Where on earth have you been?! We've been calling and texting you for hours!" She glances sheepishly at Dawson before returning her focus to me. I'm not sure if she thinks this act is fooling anyone, but it honestly just makes her look stupid.

"I can't believe you would just take off and ignore everybody like that. We've been worried sick," Dawson pipes up, glaring me down.

A chuckle escapes before I can stop myself. "Yeah, you both sounded soooo worried when you came in the door," I say, rolling my eyes at them. "Look. I'm not stupid. I just wanted to get my stuff and then I'll be out of your hair. You're welcome to continue playing house all you'd like without me," I finish, hopping down off the bar stool and heading for our bedroom. Or his bedroom rather. Maybe theirs. Hell, I don't know anymore.

"Jade, wait! What the fuck is going on?!" Emily yells, following a few steps behind me.

"Right. Like I didn't see the messages between you two this morning. It's cool. I totally get it. As I said, you're welcome to keep playing house but I won't be here for it any longer," I say, keeping my back to her as I throw some clothes into a duffel bag, along with a few essentials.

"It's not what you think, Jade. I swear!" She has tears rolling down her cheeks. She's always been such a great actor. Really missed her calling truthfully. We've been friends long enough that I know those are entirely fake though. Even if they were real, I just don't have any sympathy for either of them anymore.

Pushing past her, I run into Dawson in the hall. "I'll find a place this weekend and have your key back to you by Sunday evening."

"Jade, wait. You've got this whole thing all wrong. There's nothing going on between me and Emily."

"Okay. Whatever. Like I said, I'll have the key back by Sunday evening," I state again, brushing by him and to the front door. Once it's closed, I sigh, releasing all the pent-up emotion from my lungs. Before the tears have time to spill over, I've got the duffel bag slung over my shoulder and am heading away from the house, leaving it and them in the past.

***

"What can I get ya, sweetheart?" the waitress questions. She's petite, dirty blond, and country as the day is long, although that accent is definitely overexaggerated to earn some extra tip money. People love a thick country southern accent around here.

Sliding the menu to the edge of the table, I give her my order and all but collapse against the vinyl back of the booth. I'm exhausted but trying to hold it all together for now. I've got to get a game plan together and falling apart in the middle of an old school diner just isn't going to help that process along.

I made a quick stop to get a new phone as soon as I left the house, complete with a new number. After the basic set up, I set my mind to finding a new place to live for now, even if it's just something temporary. Unfortunately, the rental market in this town sucks about as much as the people do.

21

By some miracle, I stumble on an ad for a small one-bedroom apartment that isn't priced sky high. It isn't in the greatest part of town, but that doesn't really matter so much right now. It's got a roof and a couple walls and that's all I really need at the moment.

I dial the number and set up an appointment in two hours to swing by and look at the place, knowing that doesn't make a difference. I'm going to have to take the apartment regardless.

The waitress is back with my burger and fries, pulling me from my thoughts just before the tidal wave made landfall. Thank the heavens because that one was sure to drown me. Everything changed in the blink of an eye, and I'm struggling to process it all.

"Thank you so much," I say, picking up a fry. With a tight smile, she turns and heads back to the kitchen, continuing her day like nothing has changed. Like the world hasn't turned to chaos and collapsed. But I guess for everyone else, it really hasn't changed a bit. It just feels like the end of the world for me today.

I manage to eat most of the burger, which was absolutely delicious, and some of the fries before my thoughts manage to creep back in. Once they do, I quickly pay for the food, leaving a tip on the table, and head out toward the new apartment. Time to start my new life, I suppose.

On the way there, I'm able to calm my thoughts, starting to process everything that has happened in the last

24 hours. I lost my fiancé, who I thought was the love of my life. I lost my best friend, who I thought would always be by my side and have my back, even when no one else in the world did. I lost my house, which I loved with everything in me. I spent so much time and put so much love into that place, just to have to start over somewhere new.

Yeah, but you walked out of there with your dignity and self-respect intact. That's gotta mean something, right? I think, doing my best to see the bright side. *Plus! That means you get to decorate the new place however you want. No more arguments about accent walls!* That brings a tiny smile to my face, brightening the day slightly. Maybe I can do this after all.

Before I know it, I arrive at the leasing office. A bell chimes as I step through the door, letting the manager know someone has arrived.

"Well, hello! You must be my one o'clock viewing! I'm Marge, the manager here at Creekwood," the bubbly, tiny woman rushes.

"I'm Jade," I provide, feeling her aura permeate the space around us. Just being in her presence makes the world seem a little brighter. It's nearly obnoxious, but it does lift the spirit a bit if I'm being entirely honest.

"What a pretty name! Let me grab these keys and we'll head up to the apartment. You're going to love it! By the way, we have laundry in each unit. There's a small sauna and a pool in the back. Nothing fancy, but it gives the residents a little something to do around here," she explains, grabbing a set of keys from the desk. "There's also parking available on the side of the office, off of the main road."

"All that sounds great," I say, not really caring about any of those details at the moment. I'd really just like a place to live at this point. That's the first major step. All the little things can come later, once I'm finally settled in again.

She leads me out of the office, around a corner, and up a flight of stairs. This side of the building is facing the main street of town with the mountains showcased in the distance. Marge stops at the third door on the right. Apartment 205. The door swings open, allowing me to step inside.

I look around in surprise. This wasn't what I was expecting at all. It's brightly lit from the natural light pouring in through the living room windows. From the front door, we step directly into the kitchen. It has a large island, fridge, dishwasher, and tons of cabinet space to the right. There's a coat closet on the left. Straight in front of me is the living room with huge picture windows and a door, leading to a small private balcony with a view of the lake with more mountains behind it. Also to the right is the master bedroom and attached bathroom.

I'm stunned at how big the bedroom is. The wall to the left is similar to the living room with tons of windows. To the right is the bathroom and a decent sized walk-in closet.

"This place is so much bigger than I was expecting for the price," I say, half to Marge and half to myself. Walking out of the master, I head for the other side of the apartment, where I find a half bath, laundry nook, and another decent sized storage closet.

"I'm glad you like it!" Marge pipes in cheerfully. "The apartments here don't come open often, but they tend to impress the new tenants every time. It's hard to find this kind of space around here."

"I'll take it," I blurt out, although that was pretty obvious at this point. I'm already imagining all the ways to decorate this place.

"Oh, wonderful! Let me run down and get the paperwork together for you. Meet me back in the office when you're finished looking around, and we can get everything squared away," Marge exclaims, clapping her hands together. "I just know you're going to love it here!"

With a sigh and a huge smile plastered across my face, I hold my arms out and spin in a quick circle, letting out the stress of the day. Maybe everything is going to be alright after all. Maybe, just maybe, new beginnings aren't always a bad thing.

After another minute or two of looking around, picturing where everything will go and making a mental list of things I'll need to purchase, I head down to the office to sign the paperwork with Marge. Within ten minutes, she hands me the keys and copies of the paperwork, along with phone numbers for the office and the maintenance crew, just in case.

In under an hour, I manage to hire a couple local guys to move the heaviest of my things from the old place and head back there to start packing up my smaller things. This is going to be amazing, I decide, setting my mind on the positives of the situation.

***

Two days later, I'm finally starting to really settle into the new place. Things are mostly put away, only a few random boxes here and there to sort through. After a long day of unpacking and organizing, I head to the shower, ready to wash away the dirt and grime, both physical and mental.

While going through the motions of my shower, my mind begins to wander, trudging through the last week's events. I sent my manuscript off to an editor, who I never got a response from, lost my fiancé and best friend, found a new incredible apartment, and started my life over from scratch. It has definitely been a rollercoaster of a week, but things are starting to look up finally.

With a small smile, I start to shut off the water but the handle is stuck again. It's been giving me some issues, but nothing major. I push a little harder, willing it to shut off, but instead, the handle snaps, causing me to slip. Trying to keep myself from splattering across the bathtub floor, I make a pathetic attempt to catch myself, breaking the faucet off the tub in the process.

I squeal when the water immediately starts spraying from where the faucet was only a moment ago. "Fuck, fuck, fuck!" I yell, trying to replace the faucet and fix the issue, which doesn't slow the water in the slightest. Tossing the useless faucet to the floor, I sling a towel around my body and shuffle to the kitchen, trying not to slip on the tile floor.

I find the number for the maintenance guy, find my phone, and make an incredibly pathetic but desperate phone call.

"Hello?" the man answers, sounding half asleep.

"Hi. Oh my god, I'm so sorry. I'm the new tenant at Creekwood. In apartment 205? I fucked up," I rush, not sure how to explain what the fuck just happened.

"What? New tenant?" he repeats, sounding slightly more awake now. "What happened?"

"Well, I was showering. The handle has been a little tricky, but it was worse tonight. So I pushed a little harder and the stupid thing snapped right off! Which caused me to slip, obviously. I tried to catch myself, but that didn't work. I landed on the faucet and it snapped off, and now there's water shooting out everywhere and I don't have slightest clue what to do!" I nearly scream, half panicking from embarrassment and half from the situation in general.

I hear a chuckle from the other side of the phone. "Alright, I'll be there in five," he says before ending the call.

I feel the heat creeping up into my face from embarrassment. *I swear, this stupid shit only happens to me.*

I hear a knock at the door in less than two minutes, catching me a little off guard. I open the door and falter, stopping dead in my tracks, nearly dropping my towel. Holy. Fuck.

The man is drop dead gorgeous. He's fairly tall, around 6'3". Jet black hair, a little shaggy and mussed up, confirming that he was asleep when I called. Long, dark lashes surrounding the most gorgeous eyes I've ever seen. They look identical to the ocean on a stormy day. A little blue, a little grey, and the smallest hint of green. And they're currently lit up in amusement at my situation.

My face turns cherry red and heats to a level similar to what I'd imagine hell being as I grab onto the towel for dear life and step back to let him into the apartment. I just thought the whole shower incident was embarrassing. I'm making a whole ass fool of myself right now and can't seem to stop it from happening to save my life.

With a smirk, he steps past me, heading straight for the bathroom. As he walks through the bedroom, I hear him clear his throat to hide full out laughter. Stepping into the room, I'm mortified when I realize I had laid out some sex toys on the bed for after my shower and completely forgot about them. *Oh. My. Fuck. I'm going to jump off a fucking bridge, I swear to God.* My breath catches in my throat, freezing me in place.

Tossing the cover back to hide the toys he's obviously already seen, I head into full blown panic mode. My body is on fire from the inside at this point. I'm not sure if I want to go jump off the balcony or go play in traffic, but death is the only viable option now.

"Okay, I shut off the water, so that fixes the main issue here," he says, doing his best to maintain his professionalism. "I don't have the parts to actually fix the shower, but I'll pick those up from the hardware store in the morning and can have you up and running again by tomorrow afternoon." He faces me now, leaning on one arm against the door frame.

Swallowing down all my shame, I nod my head, not able to make eye contact or actually utter a single word to this Greek god of a man. Who just saw my fucking dildo laying on my bed, right after I nearly flashed him, all while he's here to fix my already embarrassing situation. Talk about awkward.

"Hey, don't worry about that. Any of it honestly. You'd be amazed at what I see in some of these apartments," he laughs, trying to brush off the whole thing as entirely normal. "I'll have you all fixed up in no time and we can pretend none of this ever happened in the first place. Although, I got a good laugh from imagining the shower incident, if I'm being entirely honest," he finishes with the most genuine smile I've ever witnessed.

"I'm so sorry. This whole thing is so embarrassing. I've always been a klutz but this is fucked, even for me," I apologize quickly. "I'm also sorry for waking you up to deal with this."

"No worries," he says in his lighthearted manner. "It's what I'm here for, after all."

When I can force myself to look back up from the floor, there's a heat in his eyes I hadn't noticed before. Or maybe I'm just imagining it, because as quick as I see it, it's gone and replaced with something more professional and closed off. Not quite so vulnerable.

"Thank you again," I manage, forcing the words out of my mouth, turning back toward the living room.

"What did you say your name was? You look familiar," he questions, following me.

"I didn't. But my name is Jade. Jade Adams." I turn to find him with an odd expression on his face, almost as if he's surprised.

"Oh, shit! Really?" He runs his hand down his face as the smile creeps back onto his lips. "I'll be damned."

Arching my eyebrow, I wait for a little more information, not sure what any of this has to do with anything.

Holding his hand out, he continues. "I'm Roman Grato. You sent me an email with your manuscript a few days ago. I reached out to set up a time to meet in person but I hadn't heard back from you."

All the breath rushes from my lungs as I put a hand out to steady myself. *You've got to be fucking kidding me.*

Chapter Four

Jade

After rushing Roman out the door, I collapse onto my bed, trying to soothe the burning in my lungs and keep my dinner down. *What the actual fuck. I'm literally going to die from embarrassment.* I feel the tears stinging the backs of my eyes and my throat starts to burn as I bring my hands up to my head, wrapping my fingers in my hair. *You've got to be kidding me.*

I finally get the balls to send my manuscript off to an editor and that editor just happens to me the maintenance guy for my new apartment?! I also just so happen to break the faucet in some freak accident and he shows up here in the middle of the night to save me, and ends up seeing my sex toys sprawled out across the bed?! This can't be my real life. I pinch myself on the arm lightly, just to double check that I'm not currently having a nightmare. Unfortunately, it confirms that I'm awake and this is very much so my real life.

Fuck.

Opening my laptop, I pull up my emails and find his response to the manuscript. I hadn't even seen it yet since everything went insane right after I sent it the other day.

Roman,

Holy fuck. I am so incredibly sorry for everything that happened this evening. I hadn't gotten a chance to read your email yet. My life kind of fell apart right after I got the guts to send you the manuscript.

Anyway, I'm sure that meeting is off the table now. Plus, I'm absolutely mortified at what happened here. So, I just wanted to apologize to you once again.

Thank you for taking the time to read the manuscript, though. I really do appreciate that.

-Jade

I hit send before my heart has the chance to explode. On an exasperated sigh, I shut the laptop and let the first tears spill over. Once that happens, there's no chance of redemption. The wave has finally landed and I collapse in on myself, curling into a tight ball on the bed, sobbing until there's nothing left for me to give.

***

27 texts.

18 missed calls.

12 new voicemails.

As I rub the sleep from my eyes with the backs of my hands, my mind struggles to focus on the screen. Nobody even has this number.

Opening the phone, I see that the calls and texts are from a familiar number. Dawson. How the fuck did he get this number? I literally just got the phone and didn't give the number out to anyone yet, other than here for the apartment. I've just been using it for Facebook and a bit of YouTube at this point. The distance has kept me slightly sane.

Clicking on the messages, I notice they get more desperate as time goes on. Especially once he sent a few and didn't get any response from me at all.

Jade, I need you to call me back.

This is important.

Jade, please! Call me back right now!

Fuck, Jade. Just answer the damn phone already! I really have to talk to you!

They continue in a similar style, the last one coming in just about an hour ago. I don't even bother to check the voicemails before I type out a quick response.

What do you need?

Before I can even lock the screen, Dawson's number is flashing on my phone.

"What?" I answer, trying to keep the venom from my tone.

"Emily is dead," he states, not even bothering to lead into it gently. The silence stretches as I try to begin to process what he just said. Everything just feels blank though, like nothing is even real right now.

"What?" I repeat, barely above a whisper. When he doesn't respond for a few seconds, I wonder if I said that out loud at all. "I'll be at the house as quick as I can," I say, ending the call before he gets a chance to answer.

Ten minutes later, I'm pulling up outside his house. Our old house. Shaking my head to clear the thoughts, I open the car door and make my way to the front door. I do my best to brace myself, not sure what to expect.

My hand touches the knob but the door is flung open, revealing Dawson on the other side. "Thank god you're here. I'm freaking out and I don't have a clue what to do," he rushes, pulling me in for a quick hug, squeezing the air from my lungs.

I push back against him, freeing myself. "Slow down. What the fuck happened? What do you mean Emily is dead? Where is she? What are the police saying? Holy hell," I word vomit, trying to keep my head from spinning. Feeling dizzy, I lean against the doorframe for some support. I'm barely remaining upright at this point.

"They're not really saying anything. That's the problem! They won't talk to me at all! They asked a bunch of questions and then basically ghosted me," he shouts, rage boiling to the surface now.

"Start from the beginning. Go slow," I instruct, hoping to find some answers. Or at least get some clarity on what's happened since I've been MIA the last few days.

"God, I really don't know, Jade," he rushes, nearly tripping over his words. It's a rare thing to see Dawson so worked up. The whole situation has me feeling like my nerve endings are all on fire.

With a deep, steadying breath, he pushes himself to continue. "Emily had been staying here the last couple nights since you've been gone. We were both worried sick about you and hoping you would call or come home. We spent hours trying to figure out a way to find you and get everything sorted out. She didn't sleep hardly at all." There are tears in his eyes, rimming them red now. I fight the urge to roll my eyes so he will keep going.

"I must have fallen asleep at some point. I woke up to this insane pounding on the door. It scared the fuck out of me. I hopped up off the couch and ran to the door, praying it was you," he pauses, giving me a second to respond. When I don't, he starts again. "It was the police. They asked if I knew Em. I told them I did, so they asked to come in. That's when they told me something terrible had happened. They had found Em dead."

"Where did they find her?" I ask, urging him on, my head spinning. My subconscious refuses to believe this is happening, that this is my real life. No amount of details from Dawson or the police is going to fix that level of denial.

"A couple hikers called it in. The couple had noticed some broken branches or something. The area just seemed off, they said. When they looked a little farther, they saw a bunch of blood and then Emily's body a little farther away. She was a little way off that tiny trail that goes to the overlook. Not the popular one. The hidden one that looks out over the prettiest part of the river," he divulges. It's like once he started talking, he couldn't stop until it was all out or he would never be able to finish telling me.

I stop in my tracks. She didn't even know about that spot. We were friends for over a decade and that spot was never mentioned. That was my spot. I swallow, trying with all my might to keep the contents of my stomach in their rightful place. My head is swimming and I can't breathe.

It had to have been someone local. None of the tourists would know about that place. It's not on any map and not many of the local people even know about it. That's what has always made it so incredible over the years. Hell, from the way the trail is grown up, it looks like nobody ever goes up there anymore at all. And now my best friend was found dead there. Murdered.

I slide along the doorframe down to the floor, no longer trusting my legs to hold me upright. Hugging my knees, I lay my cheek on them, trying to focus on breathing. My entire world is crumbling around me and I can't do anything to stop it.

"Do they have any suspects yet?" I ask, more to fill the silence than anything.

"If they do, they didn't tell me that. They were just asking general information about her. Where she lived, where she had been in the days leading up to this, her social habits," he shrugs.

"I can't think of anyone who would have wanted to hurt her. Maybe it was just a weird freak thing," I suggest, knowing in my gut that isn't right. It just doesn't sit right from the second it leaves my tongue.

"Yeah, maybe," he agrees, not sounding confident in that answer either. "I'm sure the police will get it figured out.

Murders don't happen here, so they've got all hands on deck, I'm sure."

"Let me know if you hear anything. I need some space," I reply, standing shakily and dusting off the seat of my pants. "I can't be here right now. Everything is way too overwhelming." With that, I step out the door.

I slide into the driver's seat, not having a clue where to go or what to do from here. My brain is completely empty and overflowing at the same time. It's an odd sense of drowning and watching myself drown at the same time.

Before I realize it, I'm putting my car into park and climbing out at the gym. I need some space to clear my head, and this is the best place I know of for that. Putting my earbuds in place, I hit shuffle on my playlist, letting my mind run wild.

About twenty minutes into my run on the treadmill, I'm pouring sweat and starting to lose the fire that's kept me going so far. Determined to push farther, I glance up and see Roman across the gym, watching me. With an eyeroll, and a slight falter to my pace, I refocus on the run, willing myself to ignore him. That's the last fucking thing I need today.

Ten minutes later, I'm shutting down the treadmill, swiping a towel across my sweaty forehead. I'm heading for the free weights when he steps into my path, stopping me short.

"Jade," he starts with a sly smile. "Fancy seeing you here."

"I'm really not in the mood, Roman," I spit, pushing past him. Swiping at my eye, I don't even bother to stop at the weights. Instead, I head out to the parking lot.

"Hey, what the hell?" he half yells, following me out the door. "I wasn't trying to be pushy or rude! Are you okay?" There's concern in his voice, but I'm not sure if it's for me or because he thinks he overstepped a line.

My short stride is no match for his long legs and he catches up in a few seconds, wrapping his hand around my upper arm and spinning me to face him. With tears streaming down my face, I face down the man who has already seen my most embarrassing moments. How much worse could it possibly get?

"Jade? What the fuck is going on?" he pries, voice barely above a whisper. There's an edge of concern and maybe a little pain in his tone. There's also an underlying fury that feels like it could strike a match and watch the world go up in flames, but I'm doing my best to ignore that part.

"Obviously we don't know each other well at all, but I get the feeling there isn't much that makes you cry or sends you into this kind of a frenzy. What's going on?" he repeats, rubbing my arm with his thumb gently now. I don't pull away, although all the alarm bells in my head are blaring.

I do my best to stifle the psychotic laugh that is trying to bubble its way up and out of my chest. Instead, I just put on my sweetest smile and dive right in. I'm not even sure why I'm volunteering all of this to an almost complete stranger, but once I open my mouth, the words are spewing out and I can't stop them.

"Gosh, I don't know, Roman. Maybe my fiancé and best friend were having an affair. Left that shit hole of a relationship and am on my own for literally the first time ever. I'm trying to navigate and breathe through that. Move into a new apartment and things are looking up. Until I break the fucking faucet off of my shower and have the single most embarrassing moment of my life in front of the most drop-dead gorgeous specimen of a man I have ever laid eyes on. Then! It gets even better! I wake up to a fuck ton of messages and calls this morning from said ex-fiancé, only to call him back and find out my best friend is dead! Yup, found her this morning sometime. So that's what's going on in my life lately, Roman. That's why I pushed past you and am an absolute bloody fucking mess right now," I finish, finally taking a second to catch my breath as I glare holes through him.

There's a look of complete horror on his face now. He's reeling for something to say and coming up empty. Because what the hell do you say back to that?! No words are going to be able to fix this shit storm that has become my life and he knows that as well as I do.

"Fuck," is his only response. He lets go of my arm to run his hand up through his hair. "That's a lot. No wonder you're a mess."

The look on my face must clue him in that he chose the wrong thing to say because he immediately starts back peddling as I turn toward my car.

"Damn it! That's not what I meant. I was just meaning that's a hell of a lot for anybody to deal with. It's no wonder you're crying and upset. Especially to be dealing with it all by yourself? I'm impressed that you're still even on your feet honestly," he tries, hoping to salvage the conversation.

The psychotic laugh returns in all its glory, finally making its way out into the world. Once it does, there's a small smile trying to come to life on Roman's face. Swiping at my eyes, I feel the slightest bit better. Like the world is a little lighter again.

"What the fuck am I going to do now? Jesus Christ. This is absolutely absurd," I start once the laugh dies down. "This kind of shit could only happen to me, I swear."

"Well. We could start by heading back to your place and grabbing a drink," he suggests. "We could talk through all this drama. Or maybe just get totally shitfaced and forget anything is even going on?"

"We? I thought I was doing incredibly well at handling all of this on my own, remember?" I joke, reaching out to push his shoulder playfully.

His tone takes on a seriousness that was missing a few moments ago. "You really are. I wasn't joking when I said I'm impressed with how you're handling it. I was only suggesting that perhaps it would be a little easier to keep standing if you had some support to lean on," he finishes, shrugging his shoulders slightly.

Chapter Five

Roman

Watching Jade down drink after drink, running from every demon that has ever possessed her mind, completely rewrote my definition of brave. In those moments, she was a warrior, hellbent on outrunning her past and starting over. In those moments, I started to fall for her. Irrevocably and madly.

It was in those moments I knew I would burn the world and everyone in it to keep even one more demon from ever haunting this woman. Everyone else be damned.

These were my thoughts as I carefully covered up her sleeping form on the couch where she had finally given in to sleep. She looks so peaceful now, but I know she will be back to fighting as soon as her beautiful eyes open again.

I set out some Ibuprofen and a bottle of water for her, making sure it's all within reach on the coffee table. After adding a second blanket to ensure she doesn't get too cold, I slip out the door, locking the knob behind me.

During our night, she explained what has been going on in her life recently. From the texts to the breakup to the police finding her best friend murdered on the same trail I watched her from just days ago. She cried, she screamed, and she sat silently. She laughed as she told stories from their past, getting lost in the love they used to share.

I found myself falling for her in those stories. When she would spin tales of getting blackout drunk in a random field at a bonfire, I imagined being there with her, hearing her carefree laughter. The two of them trying on their prom dresses, twirling around the store in fits of giggles. The dreams they shared of wedding days to come, of having children that grew up together as they had.

And now all of that was gone. Taken by someone else, for who knows what reason, if any at all. This woman has lost everything in the past couple days, and yet she's still upright and fighting.

That's the bravest thing I have ever witnessed.

As I walk back to my apartment, my head is filled with a million thoughts of her, mostly of reasons why I can't be falling in love with her. Alas, my heart is unfazed and I know it's no use. In just this short time, I've been completely changed and there's no going back.

"Fuck," I voice, barely above a whisper. "I'm so fucked."

Walking through the front door of my apartment, I strip off my shoes and make my way to the bathroom for a quick shower. I have a lot to do today and I'm going to need a clear head to get through all of it. It's still the middle of the night, but I'm not going to be able to sleep anyway, so I might as well be productive.

My apartment differs from the others in the building. Since I've been working here for several years, the owners have allowed me to change some things and make it more my own style.

Instead of the sterile white of the others, my apartment is darker. Black tile with silver grout in the bathroom, including the walk-in shower I had built. Most of the walls are a medium grey with a few black accent walls throughout. The floors in most of the house have been changed out to a dark grey tile as well.

It isn't much, but the personal touches I've been able to add make it feel more like home than anywhere else I've ever been. It's a small piece of stability in a life that has otherwise been complete chaos.

Once in the bathroom, I turn on the shower, which causes a smirk to slide across my face when I remember my first official encounter with Jade. Stripping down, I step into the shower, feeling the warmth spread over my back. I roll my head from side to side, starting to relax as the hot water melts away the tension between my shoulders.

Just as the soap is being rinsed down the drain, my phone starts to ring in the bedroom, pulling me from my thoughts.

"Who the fuck is calling me this late?" I wonder, caught completely off guard. Although, I'm thankful for the distraction if I'm being honest. I was getting lost in my head and that's never a good place to be with a past like mine.

Drying off quickly, I wrap the towel around my waist and half run to my phone.

"Hello?" I answer, more than half annoyed at this point. "It's two in the fucking morning," I add for good measure.

"Oh. Fuck. Um. Never mind," a small voice says before I hear the click of the call ending.

"Damn it," I berate myself before hitting redial in an attempt to fix my fuck up. I didn't even bother to look at who was calling before I answered. "Answer the damn phone," I growl, annoyed for a totally different reason now. When her voicemail picks up, I slam the phone down on the nightstand and trudge to the closet. I slip on some pajama pants and am out the door in less than a minute, leaving the phone behind.

With beads of water still dripping from my hair and running down my chest, I make my way to her apartment. I knock once, the door immediately swinging open.

"Can I help you? It's two in the fucking morning after all," she spits, voiced laced with venom. I'd be lying if I said she wasn't cute as hell with that attitude, although I'd love a chance to adjust it for her.

Apparently, the smile that covers my face isn't amusing to her in the slightest. If this were a cartoon, there would definitely be steam billowing out from her ears right now. A chuckle escapes at the thought, causing her to try to slam the door in my face. Unfortunately for her, I saw that coming and slipped my foot in the door, which will probably have a bruise now. Worth it though.

"Actually, you can. So kind of you to ask," I soothe, making my voice sweet as candy. "When I left, you were passed out on the couch. I thought you would be out for the night, but I was obviously wrong. Were you needing something when you called?"

Those gorgeous hazel eyes are rolling to the back of her head as I finish my question. "I don't need anything from anyone at this point," she spits.

"Okay, okay. That's fair," I soothe, raising my hands in surrender. "Was there something you were wanting though?" I ask, trying a new angle.

With a sigh dramatic enough to match the eye roll, she steps back and allows the door to open fully. When I don't move, she simply turns and walks away, back toward the living room. I take the invitation and quickly follow her inside, closing the door gently behind me.

I pause when I don't find her in the living room like I had expected. Instead, I see a dim light coming from her bedroom. Peeking around the corner, I find her sitting cross-legged on the bed, watching me warily.

Leaning against the doorframe, I wait for her to say something. The ball is in her court here. I'm not sure what she wanted when she decided to call me, but I'm not going to push to find out either.

Picking up a glass from the night stand, she downs the rest of the alcohol and flops back against the bed and sighs in what I can only guess is frustration.

"I don't really know why I called you," she pipes up after a few seconds, hazel eyes finding mine. "I guess I just didn't want to be alone, and I don't really have anyone else, if you hadn't noticed."

"Oh, so I'm just the person you call when nobody else is available?" I joke, feigning hurt. I even pull my hand to my chest for the dramatic effect.

She's glaring when she tries to sit upright. Her attempt is inhibited by the alcohol in her system though, so she only makes it about halfway up, resting on her elbow.

"Obviously," she states, rolling those pretty eyes again. "Come sit down. You're making it weird." With that, she collapses back against the comforter again, adjusting the pillow underneath her head. "I fucking hate everything. I really don't want to be alone tonight, but you're welcome to leave if there's somewhere else you'd rather be," she offers.

Padding softly across the room, I ease down onto the bed facing her, pulling my legs underneath me. "If you want me here, there's nowhere else I would rather be," I assure her. "Hell, even if you don't want my company, there's still nowhere else I would rather be," I add, feeling the need to be entirely honest with her in this moment.

She scoffs at that as if she doesn't believe it before throwing her arm up and across her eyes. "Lay down," she instructs bluntly.

I do as she asks, lying back against the pillow next to her, allowing her time to figure out what she needs from me. Just when it seems as if maybe she's fallen asleep, she starts talking again, her voice thick with unshed tears and barely bottled rage.

"I just can't believe I didn't see what was going on, you know? It's so obvious now," she starts, shaking her head and allowing the tears to slide down her cheeks freely. "They were always laughing and play fighting. All the stupid cliché things. I sincerely thought it was only because we were all so close. We had been friends forever."

With less than an ounce of grace, she flips over onto her side, facing me. Once the dramatic sigh has been fully released from her lungs, she continues her tirade.

"Who the fuck even does that anyway?!" she nearly shouts. "Yet I'm the one lying here feeling guilty as hell for being angry with a dead girl. Make it make sense." I can't see her well in the dim light, but I guarantee she just rolled her eyes again. I bet those things are in great shape from all the exercise she gives them.

"You have every right to be mad at her," I start gently. I'm not quite sure how to soothe the situation, but I do my best to de-escalate it a bit. "Honestly, it's going to sound harsh, but just because she's dead doesn't change what she did with your ex. She still betrayed you. You didn't lose the right to be upset about what they did just because something traumatic happened afterward."

The sob that ensues as soon as the words are out of my mouth is baffling. I'm pretty confident I did not de-escalate the situation in the slightest. "I'm sorry. I wasn't trying to make you feel worse," I say, unsure of how to proceed.

"No, you're totally right. Reality hits different when it comes out of someone else's mouth is all. The reality that my best friend is dead. The reality of what they did. My feelings about what they did and who they are to me now. All of it," she sniffles, choking against the words. It seems almost painful for her to push the words past her teeth. All the alcohol probably isn't helping that either.

Suddenly, she's bouncing up off the bed and the lamp is illuminating a small portion of the room. I slowly push up onto my elbows before sitting up all the way, wary of the situation. "You okay?" I ask cautiously.

"I just had a thought. Ya know, thinking about reality and all. I know my friends were deceiving me, but what about you?" she begins. I can see the wheels turning in her head now but can't see the direction she's heading.

"What do you mean?"

"I mean you just showed up out of nowhere. I saw you at the gym, the day I found out about Emily and Dawson," she starts, pacing across the floor, counting on her fingers. "Then, you're doing maintenance at my brand new apartment? Only for you to later throw it out that I sent you my manuscript as well?! The one I finally got the guts to send to some random editor?" She's panting now. When she looks at me, there's a storm of emotions swirling behind her eyes.

I know she's only saying all of this because of the alcohol, but honestly, she's right. There have been a lot of run-ins lately. I hadn't even realized how weird it all sounds until she laid it out like this.

"Damn. You're right," I start, trying to figure out how exactly to explain myself. "Let's start with the gym then, shall we? I've been going to that gym for years. Obviously. Have you seen my physique? This masterpiece doesn't just happen overnight," I smirk. She scoffs but I catch her eyes doing a quick once over nonetheless.

"As for the maintenance, I've been working as a maintenance tech in this building for years. When I first moved to town, I didn't have a penny to my name and nowhere to go. I happened across this building and basically begged the old lady for a place to stay for a week in exchange for doing some work here. I've always been good with my hands, and she was down on her luck with a maintenance guy. One week turned into a month. A month turned into a year and here we are," I pause, waiting to see if she has any questions up to this point. When she doesn't say anything, I continue.

"The editing thing is a little harder to actually explain I guess," I say, being entirely upfront with her. "I have a huge passion for books. I always have, ever since I was around eight years old. I didn't have a good childhood and reading was an escape for me. I would take new books home from school every week, and that was how I survived my homelife. So, when I grew up, I started writing and editing. That's my main income stream at this point. Although, I have to admit, I'm offended by being called "some random editor"," I poke, a smile pulling at one corner of my mouth.

"Fuck. I'm sorry. I didn't mean that in a bad way!" she spouts, covering her face with both hands. I can see the flush creeping up her neck, knowing my comment embarrassed her at least a little.

"It's fine," I laugh. "I was just joking. I'm not actually offended." Once she allows her hands to fall from her face, I continue. "I truly don't know how to explain all of those freak occurrences though, other than the truth. I hadn't even put all the pieces together until you brought it up just now."

"Hold up. You said you've been going to that gym for years, right?" she questions. I nod my answer. "How come I've never seen you there? I've been going four or five times a week for years now." That distrust is back in her eyes again, shadowing any of the trust we had started to build.

"I've been going about three times a week normally, just depending on the work volume. Most of my editing work and maintenance need to be done during the day, so I hardly ever go to the gym before dark. Plus, I'm not the biggest fan of interacting with other people," I supply, knowing it sounds weak.

"I guess that's fair." With that, a bit of the warmth returns to her eyes, though she's still far more guarded than she was before the thought popped into her head.
"Any other questions, madam detective?" I prod, raising an eyebrow in her direction.

She taps her forefinger against her delectable lips, as if she's digging deep for another one. "Actually, yes, *sir*," she mocks. "Why haven't I seen you around here before now?"

Her innocent eyes pull me in until I feel as if I'm drowning. Breaking eye contact is damn near painful, but I do it to regain a bit of my focus. This woman has an insane pull and that sounds like an addiction waiting to happen.

"I try to stay to myself. Like I said, I'm not much of a people person," I shrug. "I'm normally cooped up in here working all day, then hit the gym when everyone else is sleeping. There are only about 2,300 people in this town and it seems as if my old life created enemies everywhere I turn, so I don't go out anymore really."

"Your old life?" She's crawled back into bed now, covered to her waist, yawning as she leans against the headboard.

"Yeah, I was a debt collector once upon a time," I reason. It's not the entire truth, but I did collect on debts of sorts. I just hardly ever collected money is all.

"That doesn't sound so bad," she soothes. "I can see why people wouldn't like you though. Nobody likes debt collectors." Her eyes are getting heavy as she fights to stay conscious. Between the alcohol and the warm covers, it's a losing battle.

Flipping off her lamp, I quietly pad out of the bedroom, doing my best not to wake her. "You have no idea," I say to the darkness.

Chapter Six

Jade

A week after Emily's body was discovered, I shoot Dawson a quick text. Although we haven't talked much since I found out they had an affair behind my back, I don't know who else to turn to for a bit of support. Plus, I want to know if he's heard anything from the police.

J: Any news about Em?

D: Nothing. What about you?

J: Radio silence over here.

D: We should get together later this evening. Maybe have a talk?

With that, I shove my phone into my back pocket and slip on my shoes. There's no way in fuck I'm going to meet Dawson. We don't have anything else to discuss at this point, assuming he doesn't hear anything about Emily.

It's been a week without any sort of communication from the police now. We haven't heard a single thing about a potential suspect, nothing about new evidence. Nada. I'm not really sure if that means they're actually doing nothing or not, but that's how it feels and I'm fed up.

If they're not going to solve Em's murder, I will.

With that thought, I step out the door, closing and locking it behind me. Heading down the stairs, I put in one earbud and start the walk to the overlook.

I haven't been there since they found her body. I've been putting it off because I truly don't know what to expect. At this point, I'm not sure if it would bother me more to see the area all taped off as a crime scene, or completely undisturbed like nothing ever happened.

As I make my way there, my mind starts to unravel a bit. It's bouncing around like that squirrel from Ice Age, chasing a nut with all its might but never quite grasping it. By the time I'm stepping onto the path, my mind is completely blank and feeling rather numb.

When I see absolutely nothing, that's when everything hits me. I feel as though I've plunged into sub-zero waters, all the air rushing from my lungs. My head is spinning as the reality of my life crushes my soul and every shred of desire I have to keep moving forward.

As I hit my knees in the dirt where her body was discovered, I completely lose myself to the emptiness. Heart wrenching sobs rack my body until I'm shaking from head to toe, barely able to pull in enough air to keep me conscious.

The worst part of it all is that they aren't doing anything to find her killer. Whoever the bastard is, he's out there walking free, getting away with murdering one of the most integral parts of my soul.

After a few agonizing minutes, the sobs begin to subside and I pull my phone from my pocket, wiping the back of my hand under my eyes to clear the tears enough to see.

J: They aren't even trying. There's no tape. Nobody's here. Nothing.

I pull my knees to my chest, staring at the ground. I know I should probably leave, but I'm positive my legs won't hold my weight. So I sit. And I weep. Not only for Emily, but for the life I knew and the person I was before. I'm mourning two deaths, and it just might be more than I can handle.

***

I'm startled back to consciousness when I realize I'm being lifted off the ground. After a quick freak out, I catch his eyes and stop struggling so he doesn't drop me. Peering into those icy ocean eyes will never stop taking my breath. For the first time, I stare into them without hesitation, not daring break the contact. At this moment, it feels like they're the only things grounding me to the earth.

"What are you doing?" I ask, although that seems rather obvious. I just don't know what else to say to start a conversation right now.

"Rescuing you obviously," he answers, putting on his very best Prince Charming smile. It does the trick. The laugh that escapes me seems to light a fire in him, bringing warmth into his eyes.

"I'm not a damsel in distress, Roman," I say, though I'd be lying if I said I wasn't enjoying being treated like I needed saving right now. Hell, maybe I do, now that I think about it.

"Either way. You didn't answer your phone when I texted a while ago, so I came to find you. Somehow I kind of figured you would be here," he answers the questions forming in my head before I even realize they needed to be asked.

"Oh. Sorry," I nearly whisper. "It wasn't intentional." I feel the tears burning the back of my throat again. Pulling my phone from my pocket, I open the screen to see several messages and a couple missed calls. "You can put me down now, you know? I can walk from here," I say. He gently places me on my feet after a moment of hesitation.

I immediately miss the warmth of his body pressed against mine, regretting my comment already. I shiver as my arms are quickly coated in a layer of goosebumps from the sudden chill. It doesn't escape him, and he looks quite satisfied with the way my body reacts once his is no longer wrapped around me.

Rolling my eyes at him, I look back down at my phone.

D: You've got to give them time, Jade. They can't fix everything in just a couple days. They'll find him.

The text does little to soothe my fury at how little progress there has been. It doesn't appear that anything is really being done, like she was swept under the rug when it wasn't super obvious who her killer was. You'd think it would kill them to put in a little effort from the way they're acting.

I don't bother to text him back. Obviously, we don't feel the same way about the situation, so that leaves very little to talk about anymore. With an exasperated sigh, I slip my phone back in my pocket once more and find curious eyes focused on my face, reading my expressions.

"It was nothing. Dawson just telling me to be patient and the police will eventually do their job," I answer, though

I don't know why I'm even telling him anything about what's going on. He didn't even know Em.

"Oh. Maybe he's right," he shrugs. "Doesn't really seem like it from what you've told me and what I just saw at the overlook though."

"Right?! Ugh, I thought it was just me being uptight because it was personal for me!" I squeal, relieved that someone actually agrees with me. "I feel like there's got to be something more they could be doing. If I had a clue where to even start, I swear I would find the guy who did this and end him myself."

"Well... I'm sure a call to the police station wouldn't hurt. Maybe you could find out where they stand on everything and what's being done to find the guy," he suggests. "Then if you're not satisfied, you could call around or something and see if you can get any leads of your own."

"That's a great idea!" Suddenly there's a fire in my chest and I feel as though I have a reason to keep breathing again. Her killer has to be brought to justice, one way or another.

***

"Yes, sir. I understand. Thank you so much," I say, clicking the end button. Slumping back against the couch in my apartment, I rub the heels of my hands into my eyes gently before dropping them back onto the couch in frustration.

Roman walked me back here after we left the overlook and wanted to stay while I made the call to the station so I didn't have to face that alone. "Fuck."

"No luck?" Roman hands me a cup of steaming coffee, the room quickly filling with the delicious hazelnut scent.

"Not really. He basically said they've come to a dead end unless there's some sort of breakthrough. These things just don't happen here and they don't have the resources to delve any deeper into it without any sort of evidence or anything," I repeat, giving him the same story the detective just gave me.

"Okay. Now what?"

"What do you mean 'now what'? They don't have any leads. There's nothing to do except sit and wait apparently," I say, more than a little frustrated.

"Hold up. That doesn't sound like the Jade I've come to know. You can't give up on her that easily. Nobody else is going to solve this unless it just falls right into their lap. Is that what she deserves?" he questions, no doubt in an attempt to motivate me, but all it does is piss me off.

"Actually, yeah. Maybe it is. It turns out she was a shitty person anyway. Why should I even give a fuck if they ever find out who killed her or not?" I question, venting my anger out to him, tears once again burning the backs of my eye.

"You have a point there," he shrugs. "She did a really terrible thing. Something that I can only imagine caused you an incredible amount of pain. And honestly, I wouldn't blame you if you gave up on it and said fuck it. You just need to decide if that's something you can live with or not. I've got your back either way," he finishes. That one does the trick though. I think he knows me well enough by now to know that would hit me differently. It isn't really about Em anymore. This is about me and living out the rest of my life. I need to know who did this and see the justice served. This is about what I can live with and what I can't.

"Fucking hell. I hate you," I seethe, giving him my very best death glare, which only causes him to burst into a fit of laughter. After he's able to contain himself again, I ask, "So what now? How do I even start on figuring this out?"

"I can ask around here? See if anybody has heard anything? You know how people in these tiny towns love to gossip. Surely somebody has heard something by now. That might give us a starting place," he offers.

"Us?"

"Us. I told you I have your back, no matter what you decide. Plus, I got good at finding out dirt on people when I was a debt collector. We'll find out if I'm rusty or not yet," he winks, somehow making me feel more at peace than I have in quite some time. And I'm not entirely sure how I feel about that.

"Okay," I agree. "You ask around and see what you can find out. I'll update Dawson and figure out my next step."

J: Police know nothing. Finding the bastard myself.

D: We really need to talk. It's important, Jade.

Blowing him off yet again, I put my phone on the table and head to my room to write down everything I know so far. Maybe there's a clue somewhere in all of this that will give me some kind of lead or somewhere to start at least.

Chapter Seven

Roman

Something about Emily's murder just isn't sitting right with me. I haven't been able to completely shake this feeling since Jade told me what happened. Going over all the details she has been given so far, there's definitely something that doesn't quite add up, but I can't put my finger on it. Who would have it out for such a beautiful young girl, with no obvious enemies? She's just really starting her life, so she hasn't had much time to make that kind of an enemy honestly.

Then to take her to a spot that's so unpopular that few people know about it? That's the part I keep getting hung up on. Hell, I've lived in this town for years and just recently learned of the place myself. That in and of itself makes the act feel personal. Maybe a jaded lover? An ex who was a little too controlling or narcissistic? Seems a bit extreme, even for that type of person though.

There's always the possibility it was entirely random. But once again, the area her body was found in rules that out. It's highly improbable a random person would have dumped her body there. That was intentional.

Fuck. I'm racking my brain and absolutely nothing is coming from it. I'm missing several pieces still. There's no way I'm going to solve this puzzle without some further investigation. So, I slip on my shoes and head out to do exactly what I said I was going to do. As much as I hate talking to people, there's no better way to start in this case.

***

"Right. I completely understand. Well, thanks for talking with me anyway," I finish, now having talked to four people in the building but coming up short. Nobody here has seen or heard anything about the murder. Just the same details that were released to the public in the press conference, plus some small town speculation.

"Hold on a second," she stalls, stopping me in my tracks. Even as an older woman with greying hair, petite frame, and sickly appearance, she has a commanding presence. There's an air of authority that clings to her small body. A tad hesitant now, she continues after looking around to make sure nobody can overhear us. "I might know somebody who can help you out. I'm not sure if she knows anything or not, but she would be my go-to in this kinda situation. She has resources in this town like you wouldn't believe. Wait right here," she says, slipping back inside her apartment, softly closing the door behind her.

I'm growing more impatient by the second now. Just when I think she's not coming back, she opens the door a few inches, handing me a slip of paper with a phone number on it. No name.

"Tell her Patsy told you to call," she instructs.

"Yes, ma'am," I comply. "I certainly will. Thank you so much for your help."

"I haven't been of any real help, young man, but Sara may be able to help you along. I want to know who murdered that young lady and why just as bad as everybody else in this town. These kinds of things just don't happen here and it has everybody on edge," she confides. "Find out what happened to her so we can all rest a little easier." There's a softness to her tone that has my heart aching. She's terrified, and so are a lot of other people apparently.

With that, she steps back inside the apartment before quietly closing the door again. I hear the soft click of the lock sliding into place as I take a step back toward my apartment.

Five minutes later, I'm leaning against my kitchen counter, dialing the number I was given. Hoping against hope that this is at least a starting place, I hit send on the call, not wanting to waste any time. The call seems to ring for minutes, though I'm sure it's no more than fifteen seconds or so. Just when I'm about to hang up, the line connects and I hear a woman on the other end.

"Hello?" she questions, her voice full of frustration.

"Hey. I got your number from Patsy. She said you might be able to help me out with some information," I say, jumping right to the point. Just from that one word, I would bet Sara isn't the patient type.

"If you got my number from her, we shouldn't be having this conversation over the phone. I'll meet you at Broadstone in an hour." Without waiting for a response, she ends the call, leaving me staring at my phone in my hand.

What the fuck have I gotten myself into? I wonder, letting my imagination run for a few minutes. This doesn't sound like anything I want to be mixed up in, but I promised Jade she wouldn't deal with it alone, and I fully intend to keep that promise, come hell or high water.

***

I've been to this park a thousand times, but it feels different this time. The air feels thick, like it's hard to pull it into my lungs. Everything seems dreary, as if there's something deeply amiss, although no one seems to notice or be affected by it aside from myself.

I head over to the creek, trying to avoid the people here just trying to relax or play with their kids. Laughter and chitchat fill the air. I do my best to drown it all out, making it nothing more than a little background noise. My head is still trying to wrap itself around everything going on and the reason for my visit.

Sitting on the bank, I pull my shoes and socks off, placing them neatly beside me before I dip my feet into the crystal-clear water, noting that I can clearly see each rounded rock as my feet ripple the water. It's a nice contrast to the hot and sticky day. Without much thought, I decide to wade in a little way, about mid-calf deep, thankful I wore shorts today.

"Enjoying yourself?" she asks, making me jump and causing my feet to slip on the moss-covered rocks along the creek bed. I was so lost in thought; I didn't even hear her arrive. I right myself within seconds, but my breath is still rapid, heart still hammering inside my chest.

Willing my racing pulse to slow down, I take in the sight of her. She's about 5'7" or so, average build, wearing black from head to toe, including an incredible twisted Alice in Wonderland shirt that sports Alice licking a knife while the Cheshire Cat lazes on a mushroom behind her, beaming with pride. It goes well with the bright purple shoulder-length hair, piercings, and tattoos.

She sits gracefully beside my shoes, legs folded beneath her, waiting for me to climb out of the creek and plant myself on the ground facing her.

"What can I help you with?" she questions genuinely, her southern drawl pulling me in. "It's not often Patsy gives my number to strangers, so it must be important."

"What do you do exactly? She didn't give me anything to go on. Just your number on a piece of paper. Said to call and you could help me." I don't exactly trust this woman, though she's given me no reason not to. Her accent reminds me of an old southern grandmother. The kind who would welcome just about anyone into their home, not a care in the world. It's a façade though, at least partially. That accent could easily lull someone into a fall sense of security, like she's a harmless, innocent young woman. She's sweet but not a person I would want to cross on the wrong day.

"Well. I grew up here but always had bigger dreams. I never wanted to live out my life here, but somehow, I keep coming back. When I was in high school, I took an interest in computers. Coding and all that fun stuff. The geek type stuff. Turns out, I'm pretty exceptional at finding out people's secrets," she shrugs, as if it's the most normal thing in the world. "I mostly do surveillance for bigger companies now. Make sure their cameras are all up and working properly. Occasionally, I help people find answers they wouldn't be able to get otherwise."

I take a minute to process everything she has offered me, letting the laced silence hang between us. I'm half hoping she will keep talking, half hoping she doesn't. Truth be told, the less I know about this woman, the better off I'll be if things go south.

Realizing I don't have much to lose, I share the information I do have with her, aware that every detail I have has been released to the public already. I relay everything Jade has told me, along with my own thoughts about the situation. I tell her about my gut feeling, about something just not adding up, though I can't quite place what it is.

"You said there was blood everywhere?" she repeats, making sure she has all the details written down.

"That's what they said. They didn't give any real details on how she died, no cause of death. I haven't heard any conclusion on an autopsy, though I tried contacting the police about that myself. It's still underway apparently. So I'm not sure if that's from the struggle or if she was stabbed or what happened exactly." I rehash a few more small details with her before she's standing, brushing the dust off the back of her pants.

"I don't have enough details yet to say what the issue is with this story you all have been fed, but I'll do some digging and see what I can find out. Maybe make a few phone calls. I'll be in touch in a few days. Sooner if I find something interesting. In the meantime, I need you to keep her talking. Keep her close in case new details come up from her side. If they do, you know how to reach me," she says. Her eyes are full of sorrow, almost like she feels the burden personally. Like she needs to help people find the answers so they can have a little peace and closure, knowing the truth.

"Thank you so much for all your help. I appreciate it more than you could ever know. If there's ever anything I could do to begin to repay the favor, just make it known," I say, holding her gaze for a few extra seconds.

With an almost imperceptible nod, she turns and slowly walks the other direction, back toward the entrance to the park. I let out a heavy breath, feeling the weight settle onto my shoulders. Although I know it's not my burden to bear, I have to find out what happened to Emily. I have to find that peace for Jade.

With a sick feeling taking root in the pit of my stomach, I head back home, feeling more defeated than hopeful.

I'm feeling restless, but for now, all I can do is keep a close eye on her and make sure she's safe.

It isn't long before I'm twisting the key in my front door, slipping through and kicking off my shoes in the entryway. Without a moment's hesitation, I open the laptop I left on the kitchen island. With a few clicks, the screen comes to life and I put my head down, burying myself in an overdue manuscript.

Chapter Eight

Jade

4:03AM.

Stretching my sore muscles, I try to piece together my evening while absentmindedly staring at the red blocky numbers on the clock on my nightstand. I remember getting into bed with a new book, strawberry daquiri in hand. I refilled the glass a few times, effectively finishing off the bottle. I remember being distracted and not really able to retain what I was reading. My next conscious moment was opening my eyes to those blocky numbers, body feeling heavy from the deep sleep.

All I can remember now are hazy dreams of Emily, seeing her face when we were kids, streaked with dirt and sweat, laughing and soaking up the summer sun. Dreams of our wedding days, the children we would raise together, and all the future goals between us. Those dreams quickly turned to nightmares as they were invaded with horrific scenes of blood and gore. The trail where she was found, the last few days of unanswered questions. I've been reliving it all in graphic, morbid detail every time I manage to fall asleep. The monster who took her from me is always there, but he's hazy and out of focus on the outskirts.

Rubbing the sleep from my tired eyes, I feel around for my book, slipping the bookmark in to the last page I remember reading. After stumbling to the bathroom to relieve my aching bladder, I shuffle back to the kitchen for a glass of water and some toast, hoping to ease the morning hangover a bit.

Opening my phone, I'm greeted by several new messages. One from my mom back home, begging me to call and update her when I get the chance. Letting me know she's worried about how I'm handling things. Blah, blah, blah. With an annoyed sigh, I scroll to the next message.

R: Hey, sunshine. Let's catch up later. Wanna make sure you're still breathing.

R: Ah fuck! That was inconsiderate. And awful. And rude. Fuck.

R: Sorry...

With a half-smile, I roll my eyes at his awkwardness. It's almost endearing. It really does add to his charm to see him slightly uncomfortable when everything else about him seems so confident and self-assured.

J: What a prick.

J: Just kidding. I'll call you later so you'll have proof I'm still alive lol.

I make my way through the rest of the messages quickly, stopping when I see another text from Dawson. My earlier smile drops in an instant. He's been adamant about meeting up to talk for the past several days, though I've been avoiding him completely. I just don't have the mental space to deal with his bullshit right now, but it might be easier to just have the conversation and be done with it at this point.

J: Meet me at noon. The café.

Tossing my phone to the counter with a thud, I make my way back to my bed, determined to get some work done.

It's been days since I've even read my emails, let alone written a single word.

Five minutes into emails, I've already seen three rejection letters from editors. Skimming each one, I mentally catalog them to respond to later. With my mood quickly tanking and tears filling my eyes, I shut down the email, clicking back over to my latest project and begin to reread the last section with a lump in my throat.

I've spent the last decade writing religiously, though you'd never guess it from the insane number of rejections I've received. All these years, my only real goals have been to settle down and write a best-selling novel. It seems like both of those dreams have gone up in billowing smoke recently.

With all the recent distractions, my writing, and therefore my mental health, have been plummeting rapidly. Using writing for an escape from reality has always been my go-to, so I dive back in headfirst, barely pausing to take a breath it seems.

As the scene spills out on the page before me, my brain goes quiet. At least concerning my real life. I'm completely immersed in my fantasy world, character building, and plot expansion, leaving no room for Emily or Dawson, or even Roman. Nothing else matters when the words are flying from my fingertips at this rate.

Out of nowhere, my phone is blaring the scream at the beginning of Bat Country by Avenged Sevenfold, causing me to let out the most ear-piercing shriek that's ever come from my body. "Fuck!" I swear, holding my hand to my chest in an effort to keep my heart from exploding from my body. I let out a deep exhale to try to calm my racing pulse before I make my way to the kitchen to turn off the alarm.

Mentally berating myself for the song choice, I slip on my shoes and grab a water from the fridge. It's time to go meet Dawson and see exactly what the fuck is so important.

***

At noon on the dot, I take a seat in the corner booth at the little café in the center of town. The leather is cracked and chipping from years of use. This used to be our go to spot. We visited often throughout our relationship, both with and without Emily. Now those memories are all tainted, but it seemed like the right place for this meeting when I sent the text. Things started here, so it seemed fitting for them to end here as well. Now I'm not so sure.

But it's too late, as I see Dawson swing open the door and hear the little bell chime above it.

I'd been wondering how it would feel to see him, knowing the things I now know but also having had some time to process Emily's death and the utter chaos of the recent days. And all I feel is disgust. Gut-wrenching nausea, to be exact. He smiles when he finds me in the booth, causing bile to burn the back of my throat. His smile falters when it isn't returned, and something sinister flashes in his eyes. It's gone before I have time to process what I saw.

Doing my best to keep my face neutral, I wait for him to slide into the booth before folding my hands on the worn tabletop, keen to get this over with as quickly as possible.

"It's good to see you, Jade," he starts, the sadness evident in his tone. His voice is laced with it, but it doesn't have the effect on me I had expected. Instead, a deep-seated anger starts to bubble in my chest.

The anguish doesn't sound sincere, though I can't pinpoint exactly what makes it feel off. His words strike me as nearly theatrical. Like he's putting on a performance.

"What did we need to discuss?" I question, voice clipped.

"Jesus Christ. Can't even tell you it's good to see you," he says, causing my blood to boil. I sit in silence, schooling my face and demeanor as to not give anything away. Indifference is best when dealing with Dawson. He's always been one to use even the tiniest of details against you when it suits his needs. "I wanted to talk to you about Emily," he finally reveals, effectively stealing my breath.

"She's dead," I deadpan. No emotion behind the words, though I can feel the sadness as it stings the backs of my eyes and I'm sure he can see it as well.

"She is. I just wanted to talk. I know I'm the villain here. Obviously. I fucked up. We fucked up, Emily and me. None of that should have ever happened, and we never meant for it to go anywhere. You've got to believe that, Jade," he says, placing his hands on the tabletop before trying to take my hand in his. He looks hurt when I pull my hand away as if any contact will sear my skin.

"Okay," I respond, locking my icy gaze with his.

"Okay?" he asks, confusion warring with hope in his eyes.

"Yeah," I repeat. "Okay." I pull in a breath, focusing on making my face as lifeless as possible. "We done here then?"

"Umm. No? I don't know. I didn't expect you to just say 'okay' that easily. You know we didn't mean for anything to happen or for it to hurt you, right?" he doubles back, reiterating his point.

"I know you didn't mean to get caught, Dawson. You didn't mean to fuck up," I say calmly, standing from my seat. "Goodbye, Dawson."

"Jade! Don't do this," he nearly yells, standing from the booth as I reach the front door. "Fucking hell! She wasn't who you thought she was, Jade!" His plea hits me as the door closes behind me, symbolically and literally cutting us off from each other.

As I walk, my head is spinning with emotion. Really, it's the whiplash from one emotion to the next that has me feeling like I'm drunk on a carousel. From completely numb, to soul crushing pain, then back to numb. By the time I make it to his door, I don't know which way is up anymore, my entire world feeling like the axis has shifted.

I raise my hand to knock, but Roman opens the door and pulls me into his embrace before my fist ever makes contact. The warmth of his body pressing against mine has me collapsing, my legs no longer holding me upright.

Bending, Roman scoops his arm under my knees as I cling to his neck. I'm enveloped in his scent instantly. Woodsy but clean. Masculine but not overbearing. Sandalwood and sage. The familiarity pushes me over the edge and has me dissolving into sobs in seconds.

He uses his foot to gently push the door closed as he carries me to his bed, soothing me with whispers of affirmation. That he isn't leaving me. I'm safe here. We'll find out what happened to her. Laying me gently on the thick comforter, he leaves the room, coming back with a glass of wine only moments later. Glass in one hand, bottle in the other.

"Tell me all about it," he soothes, settling some deeply deprived part of my soul. With a heavy sigh, I recount the events of the day, spilling my deepest thoughts all over his bed in hopes of regaining some clarity and semblance of normalcy.

Chapter Nine

Roman

It's been three days since that night in my apartment. She asked for some time to piece things together and settle things emotionally the last time we spoke.

I've been trying to grant her that time, but it hasn't been easy.

She's occupied my brain damn near every second of every day since she left my apartment that morning. The last night we spent together, she spilled her soul here in my bed, bearing all her worries and stresses. I could see the fear swirling in her eyes, feel it in the marrow of my bones. She's terrified, and that was enough to have my heart splintering.

To keep my hands and mind busy, I've spent the last couple days combing through her manuscript. I've got to say, it's pretty extraordinary for a debut author. With some minor plot changes here and there, fixing some typos and inconsistencies, I seriously think she could have a real winner. Maybe not a New York Times Bestseller just yet, but a strong debut novel for sure.

My phone starts to buzz on the desk beside my laptop, drawing my attention away from the screen. I ignore it, hellbent on finishing these manuscript edits for Jade, thinking it might take her mind off of everything going on for a while.

The vibrating stops for a few seconds before it's starting up again. With an exasperated sigh, I answer the call, crushing the phone to my ear and snapping, "Hello?" into the speaker.

"Well don't you just sound like a Georgia peach? Sweet as honey," she drawls from the other side of the line, amusement clear in her tone. "I've been pretty busy over the last few days and thought you might be interested in what I've managed to find out so far."

When she doesn't elaborate further, I exhale the breath I was holding captive. "Name your time and place," I say, not wanting to waste another second. A sense of unease unfurls in the pit of my stomach.

"The picnic tables at Broadstone in two hours," she states, leaving no room for opposition of any kind. Without another word, the line goes dead, and I'm left staring at the phone as my thoughts begin to spiral.

I consider texting Jade, filling her in on everything. But really, what do I have to say at this point? That I met this insane stalker woman who can dig up people's dirtiest secrets through an elderly lady with a thin and fragile appearance but the air of so much more?

Deciding that would make me sound as sane as the Mad Hatter, I slide my phone back onto the desk before making my way to the shower. My mind isn't in the edits anymore, now whirling with questions and hopes about this meeting with Sara. That queasy feeling is growing in the pit of my stomach, gnawing at my insides.

Stripping off my shirt, I toss it into the overflowing hamper in the corner of my dimly lit bedroom. Looking around the room, I realize just how messy the apartment has gotten. With everything going on, cleaning has been the last thing on my mind and it shows. Scrubbing my left hand down my face, I use my right to unbuckle my belt, pulling it smoothly from the loops before tossing it onto the bed.

Pulling off my dark jeans and boxers next, I make my way to the shower. Turning the handle to hot, I catch my reflection in the mirror, taken aback at the dark circles that have formed under my eyes. There's stubble across my face now, unshaven for a few days. I look as exhausted as I feel.

Nah, I look like shit. This whole thing is taking more of a toll on me than I've wanted to admit. Grabbing the razor,

I slather shaving cream along my cheeks and quickly remove the hair. Using the hand towel to remove the left-over shaving cream, I study my work. Satisfied, I step into the steaming shower, feeling the goosebumps rise along my arms and chest from the hot water. I melt into the stream, begging the rising anxiety to loosen its grip on my chest.

My mind jumps from thought to thought as I scrub my body, clearing away the remnants of the day. From the manuscript to the murder to Jade. Always back to Jade. Her smile, the fiery attitude, and those eyes. The more I dive into her thoughts and feelings, the less I feel like I know. Her depth is astounding, though I know she isn't fully letting me in. Her past has broken her in ways that are unimaginable, leading her to not completely trust anyone anymore. I want to watch all the people who have hurt her suffer, far beyond her level of suffering even.

Shutting off the water, I shift my focus back to the task at hand. Once I've toweled off, I wrap the black towel around my waist, leaving the bathroom. Quickly dressing in a white T-shirt, black jeans, and a pair of black tennis shoes, I grab my phone and keys before heading out the door.

In under thirty minutes, I'm sitting at the picnic tables, awaiting Sara's arrival. I'm a few minutes early, hoping to have some time to clear my mind before she gets here. The crisp fall air is refreshing, filling my lungs and lifting my spirits slightly. I love the way the leaves change colors, showcasing the beauty in death. It's always been my favorite season.

"Beautiful, isn't it?" she asks, sliding onto the picnic table bench across from me. There's a tiny hint of a smile playing on her lips, almost wistful. Her eyes are far away when she makes contact with mine, like she's in another place in her head. They clear quickly and I wonder if I imagined what I saw there.

"So, I did some digging," she begins. "Looked through some surveillance footage from the visitor's center at the overlook, talked to the staff. Nothing interesting popped up there. At least not at first," she says, pulling out her laptop. Opening a file, she turns the screen toward me. "Do you know that car?" Hitting play, the screen plays a fairly grainy video of what appears to be a newer model luxury car. It's silver and sleek. A man and woman get out of the car and head toward the trails, out of the camera view.

"No," I answer, confused. "I don't think I recognize it."

"Well. The woman getting out of the car is Emily. This video was the last I was able to find of her alive. She was found early the next morning on the trail," she continues, letting the words hang heavy between us.

"Fuck." The gravity of the situation hits me in the chest, pushing the air from my lungs. This was the last time anyone saw her alive. And whoever that guy is, he was the last person to see her before she was murdered. "There's no audio?"

"Unfortunately not. It's just a video feed. Thankfully the cameras were up and working so I had a place to start," she says. "I was able to enhance the footage enough to get a license plate number on the car. However, it was a rental from a company about an hour from here. I called the company and was able to get the name of the renter. It was rented to a 'John Black'. Pretty sure that's an alias. Just sounds fake," she continues, shrugging.

"How did you even get the name? I thought that was protected information," I question, honestly just curious about the morality of her methods.

She shrugs again. "I may or may not have told the manager at the car dealer that I was a detective here in Haven County and needed the name of the renter for 'official business'. He gave me the name pretty quick after that." This causes a sly smile to spread across her face, bringing a little light into her eyes.

"You're not a detective, though," I point out.

"Well, no, not with the police department or anything like that. I never said I was with them. Just that I was a detective, which is technically true if you ask me."

I'm a little surprised by her willingness to bend the rules, but I'm also thankful for it. We've got a lead, no matter how likely it is to be a dead end. At least it's something.

"He gave me the name and license number for the renter. As I figured, it turned out to be a fake name. The guy rented the car in cash, which normally isn't allowed, but he offered them double the regular rate, so they bent the rules for him. Which sucks for us," she says, an edge to her tone now.

"Damn it," I mutter, hitting my fist against the rough top of the concrete table. "What now?" I was feeling better, but now that hope seems to be fading as quickly as it came. Without knowing who was driving that car, we're not any closer to finding her killer.

"I was able to enhance the image a bit. It seems that she was comfortable with this guy. Is there anything that stands out to you about him?" she asks, pulling up the enhanced image. Emily is smiling at the man as she's rounding the front of the car to meet him. She looks relaxed. She definitely knew the guy and felt safe with him.

"Can you zoom in on just him without distorting it?" I ask, trying to take in every tiny detail. With a few clicks, she is able to zoom in on the guy. There isn't much to go on honestly. He's average height, build on the athletic side, wearing jeans and a T-shirt with a ball cap. There's nothing to go on from the image. At least not until I spot one small detail that might lend us a hand.

A tattoo. The guy has a tattoo peaking out from under his right shirt sleeve. It's impossible to tell what it is in this frame, so I ask Sara to move the video forward slowly. Right before he meets Emily at the nose of the car, he pushes up the sleeve to scratch the top of his arm, revealing the majority of the tattoo.

"Stop! Pause it right there. Can you zoom in on it again?" I ask, nearly vibrating from the anticipation. I can't sit still now, invading Sara's space until my face is in front of the screen, blocking her view almost entirely.

"Fucking move," she demands, annoyance clear in her voice. "I can't do a damn thing with you in my way," she explains, ignoring my protests.

Reluctantly, I take my seat beside her again. It takes what seems to be hours, though I'm sure it's only seconds, before the image has been zoomed in and enhanced again. It's still grainy, but the tattoo comes into focus. It's a beautiful piece, even if it is decorating the body of a killer.

A raven is tattooed across the top of his arm with some sort of symbols. I'm not sure what they are without the picture being clearer, but there's more than just the raven. I take a picture with my phone before shoving it back in my pocket.

"I'll ask around and see if anybody recognizes the tattoo," I say in explanation. Her sigh lets me know that wasn't needed and she understood my intentions already. "Were you able to find out anything else?" I ask, suddenly ready to be finished with this meeting. It feels as if there are ants crawling inside my veins, though I was perfectly fine moments ago.

"Not anything of importance," she says, shrugging. "Everything else came up as a dead end. A few exes, a couple disgruntled family members. Other than that, everyone I've been able to reach seemed to really love her. Which just makes this even more weird if you ask me." Her eyes are focused on the creek, just a few yards from our picnic table. As if snapping back into reality, she closes the laptop and quickly stands from the table. "I'll be in touch in a few days," she offers, locking her gaze with mine momentarily.

"Sounds good," I respond, lacking much enthusiasm now. I feel as if the energy has been siphoned from my body. It takes every ounce of willpower I have left to stand from my seat and shake hands with her. "Thank you so much for all you've done," I say, sincerely grateful for the effort she's putting in for total strangers.

"No worries. It helps me sleep at night, knowing I find closure for people. Or at least try to anyway. It doesn't always work out that way," she finishes, letting the statement hang in the air between us. "Talk to you soon." She turns and slowly walks toward the entrance to the park, rarely looking up from her feet. I watch her for a few moments before pulling my phone from my pocket.

That tattoo looks so damn familiar, but I can't quite put my finger on where I've seen it before. The all-too-familiar heavy sense of dread settles in the pit of my stomach again before I lock the screen and stand from the table, brushing off the back of my pants.

An hour later, I've gotten nowhere on figuring out what the symbols actually mean, but I've done enough research to know they're Nordic symbols of some kind. Hopefully that helps narrow down who it belongs to. I send the picture over to Jade with no explanation and start on some edits again in the meantime.

Chapter Ten

Jade

"What the fuck?" I ask out loud, even though I'm completely alone in my apartment. Opening my phone, I look at the picture Roman sent again.

R: Know this tattoo?

J: What's this about, Roman?

My mouth has suddenly gone as dry as the Sahara. I do recognize the tattoo, but I want to know what his agenda is before I decide if I'm going to tell him that or not. I stare at the screen as the bubble appears, then disappears as the new text pops up.

R: Meet me at the apartment in a half hour?

I don't bother replying but put my phone in my back pocket before slipping on my sandals. I'll be damned. If Roman is asking questions about that tattoo, I need answers. Now.

My knuckles sting as I knock on the door to Roman's apartment two minutes later. "Roman!" I half-yell. I barely notice the pain as I pound the door with the side of my fist. I'm sure it sounds like the cops trying to beat the door down from the other side but I couldn't give a fuck less at this point. My gut tells me something is off and I want answers.

"Jade? What the hell?" he asks, opening the door and narrowly escaping my fist on the downswing. "What are you doing?"

"You first," I reply, digging for my phone. "What the fuck is this all about?"

"I'm going to take that as a yes then. You definitely know the tattoo," he responds, pissing me off. I wanted answers, but I guess me coming here in a rage gave Roman his instead.

"Yes, Roman. I recognize the tattoo. Now, tell me what this is all about?" I say, pushing my way past him and into the apartment. I take a seat at the island, waiting for him to join me. When he does, he finds me with eyebrows cocked and hands folded, waiting impatiently for an explanation.

"I don't really have anything solid right now, Jade. I just needed to know if you had seen the tattoo or not. I've seen it around somewhere but haven't been able to pinpoint it. That's where you came in," he supplies, adding a small shrug to aid the innocent act he's got going on. But it's easy to see when he's lying. He gets a tiny twitch beneath his right eye, and he's definitely lying right now. There's more he's not telling me.

"Yeah. Makes total sense. That's why you're acting sketchy as hell right now," I prod, voice dripping with sarcasm.

"I'm not acting sketchy. I just needed to know if you recognized it and if you would help me out a bit by telling me who it belongs to," he offers. "It's important, but you'll have to trust me on that part for now. I don't want to give you any false hope until I know it pans out." I'm struggling to even comprehend the situation, but his eyes are so sincere as they burn into mine. His gaze is almost apologetic.

"It would be really helpful if you would just tell me what's going on, Roman. I do recognize the tattoo, but I want to know what's going on first. What are you trying to figure out exactly?" I cross my arms over my chest and do my best to avoid his eyes. It's impossible to concentrate when I get caught up in his gaze.

"I swear to you, I will explain every tiny detail of what's going on once everything is sorted out. I just don't have all the answers yet. I need you to trust me on this one. I know you haven't known me long, and men don't exactly have the greatest track record. But on everything I hold dear to me, I'm telling you the truth when I say this is important. The second most important thing I've ever been a part of actually," he says, his eyes finding mine and holding me hostage once again.

"Oh yeah? And what's number one?" I ask, half curious and half sarcastic.

"Meeting you," he deadpans, effectively stealing my breath and every shred of dignity I have as my jaw falls open before it snaps shut and my eyes narrow at him.

"I'm calling bullshit, Romeo," I say with an eyeroll, adding a sigh for some extra drama. Seconds of silence following, causing my lungs to constrict to the point of pain before I'm forced to allow my eyes to make their way back to his. What I find there shakes me to my very core.

He's being dead serious.

Swallowing nervously, I wait for him to say something. Anything at this point. The silence is heavy, consuming me whole.

"Call bullshit all you want. You can't deny the tension when we're together. I can see it written across your face every time I look at you. You can't deny what you're feeling here any more than I can. Hell, Jade, I started falling for you damn near instantly. The night you got drunk and told me about everything going on did me in. I've never seen someone be so brave. Scared, of course, and rightly so, but brave and fierce enough to tackle whatever hell was on the horizon. There's something beautiful about that and I was falling head over heels before I even realized what was happening," he admits, looking sheepish now that everything has been laid out on the table. I almost expect him to backpedal. Take it all back. But he doesn't. He just watches me absorb it all, taking in every word he spilled out before me.

Shellshocked, I sit at the island, arms still crossed, and just stare. Straight ahead, at nothing in particular, trying to comprehend what just happened.

"You don't even know me, Roman. Not really. You've only seen bits and pieces. What I've chosen to show you. You know nothing about demons and what lies beneath the surface, just waiting to rip you to shreds should you get too close. Too attached," I warn, feeling the armor around my heart slip back into place. If I'm being totally honest, I've let my guard down with him somewhat. I've gotten comfortable, and that can't happen.

"I don't give a fuck about demons, Jade! I'll gladly fight them with you, help you learn to tame them, or die in the attempt. I would rather die trying to be with you than to grow old never having that chance. Never giving *us* a chance," he declares, stunning me right back into silence.

"You have no idea what you're asking for," I warn, hellbent on getting out of this mess without any casualties.

"I have a pretty good idea. Even if I don't, I'm certain it will be a hell of a ride finding out," he continues, just as determined to change my mind apparently.

"I don't do relationships anymore," I finish, determined to be done with this conversation. "Back to the point at hand, please."

"Maybe you'll give me a chance to change that someday," he shrugs, not completely letting it go but backing off for the time being. "The point, though, was that I need you to trust me. Just for a little while. I don't know exactly how long, or how things are going to play out. But I promise to clue you in on everything just as soon as I have answers. I want them just as badly as you do right now."

"Fine. Whatever," I huff, making sure he doesn't have any doubt about how frustrated I am with him and this whole situation. "It's Dawson's tattoo. He got it about a year ago."

You'd think I just dropped a literal bomb from the expression on his face.

"Excuse me? That's Dawson's tattoo?" he stammers, completely shocked.

Chapter Eleven

Roman

"That's what she said," I tell Sara, too overwhelmed by the new information to wait for a face-to-face meeting. I grip the phone tighter, crushing it against the side of my head. "She said it was Dawson's tattoo. He got it about a year ago." I can feel the tremble in my hand as I relay the information, the realization finally sinking in.

"That would mean Dawson is the last person to see Emily alive. That we have proof of anyway. But if that was the case, why wouldn't he have said so?" she questions, echoing my thoughts. "It doesn't make any sense. Didn't he tell the police that he hadn't seen Emily that afternoon?"

"No, not exactly. He told them he and Emily had been at his house, trying to find Jade since she wasn't returning their calls. Said he fell asleep and then woke up to pounding on the door from the cops," I recount.

"This proves that wasn't true though," she continues. "He wasn't at home worried to death about Jade and where she was. He was out with Emily, doing God knows what. They didn't look worried a bit in that surveillance clip." She's getting riled up, frustrated that he is acting like a victim here when he was out living his best life without her, then lying to the police when it comes to a murder investigation to try to make him seem like a better guy. "Men like him give men a bad name," she says, face twisted with disgust.

"Just to play the devil's advocate, they could have gone back to his house after leaving the overlook, which could make the rest of his story line up," I say, hating the feel of the words in my mouth. It makes me almost nauseated to go to bat for him at all, given everything Jade has told me about the guy.

"I guess that's true," Sara confirms, the scowl returning to her face. "Fuck."

"Now what?" I question, pacing the floor in my kitchen. I've scrubbed my hands through my hair so much my scalp is sore. We have nothing solid to go on here, just that Dawson is the last person we've been able to find with Emily before she was killed.

"I have no idea. I was feeling like we kinda had this one wrapped up. Closed case, ya know?" she responds, irritation lacing her voice.

"Hey, wait. Does that video ever show the car leaving? Did they leave together, or did he leave alone?" I ask, a spark of hope in my tone.

"Neither."

"What do you mean neither?"

She sighs before answering. "It means that the video footage doesn't show anything. The car is sitting there for 37 minutes on video before it cuts to an entirely different scene. The next clip was hours later, and the car is nowhere to be found. The parking lot was completely empty when the feed came back."

"Well isn't that just convenient?" I ask sarcastically. "That's just all the more damning in my opinion."

"Mine too. I fully agree with you. But the police aren't going to, Roman. They're just going to say you have some circumstantial evidence at best," she soothes, knowing I'm running out of patience by the second.

"Police be damned! They're not doing a single fucking thing to find her killer anyway! It's time we figure this out and take care of the problem ourselves!" I shout, the sound reverberating off the walls of the kitchen. By this point, I'm pacing again, opening and closing my fist over and over, needing to release some of this pent-up anger before I explode.

"You know as well as I do that you can't do that. If there's ever going to be justice for Emily, it needs to be taken through the proper channels. Plus, if you get caught doing anything stupid, you'll be the one going to jail for the rest of your life. Not the person responsible for this," she says, her voice sounding maternal for the first time.

"Fuck! I know I can't do anything about it but I feel so helpless it's unreal! I literally can't do a single thing to speed this up or get justice for her and it's driving me insane," I confess, the rage finally boiling over. I slam my hand down on the counter, sending shockwaves up my arm, but releasing a fraction of the anger in the process, allowing me a little room to breathe again.

"I'm not sure if the surveillance will lead us anywhere further, but at least we know he was with her there shortly before she died. I've got the coroner's report being emailed over, so I'll check that out and let you know what I find there. I'm also sending the video to an acquaintance of mine to see if he can give us anything more there," she says, filling the strained silence. "Just don't do anything stupid in the meantime, okay?"

She waits for confirmation that I'll behave before the phone call is wrapped up and I'm left alone with my thoughts. Suddenly the space feels small, like the walls are closing in around me. The silence here is too much for me to handle right now.

Within a few minutes, I'm pulling the apartment door closed behind me and heading toward town. I need to put some space between me and this investigation before I legitimately lose my mind.

I find myself sliding onto an open barstool about 20 minutes later. It's just shy of 9pm so the place is still pretty empty, just a couple people at the bar and a few playing pool or throwing darts.

The bar is a small, locally owned place. I happened upon it during my first week here and have loved it since that first night. It's all worn wood and stale smoke, cheap drinks and cheap food.

After ordering a whiskey sour, my go-to drink when I need to clear my head, I glance around the bar, wondering what each person is going through today. A divorce, maybe? Death in the family? Or maybe this is just a fun night out for some of them? Hell, a first date even.

As my drink is placed on the water-stained bar top, something at the pool table closest to me catches my eye. It's dimly lit, but I could swear I saw something over there. Shaking my head slightly to rid myself of the thought, I turn back toward my drink, taking a small swig, relishing the burn as the alcohol makes its way down my throat.

I drain the first drink in a couple swallows, ordering another to follow. It's going to take a hell of a lot of alcohol to get my mind off of everything tonight.

Surveying the crowd again, spotting a few newcomers, I let my mind wonder to decidedly happier times. Times before I moved to this tiny town, before editing was my main source of income and I had to do maintenance on rundown apartments to make ends meet and have a place to lay my head at night. Back to the life I lived before.

Wrong direction. Definitely don't need to be going back there. Because the truth is, that's also the time I was the most unhappy with work. The most scared for my life every time I shut my eyes to try to get some much-needed sleep.

That's when I was a "debt collector", as I had told Jade. And in truth, that's exactly what I was. Except people never paid with cash. They paid with guns or drugs, sometimes a finger or maybe a hand. Then there were the ones who couldn't pay or had pushed their luck too far. Those were the cases I hated the most.

Those were the people who paid with their lives or the lives of the people closest to them, depending on the situation.

Those are the ones that haunt my dreams, turning every night into a nightmare. Honestly, they haunt my waking hours too. I see their faces everywhere, wonder if they have people of their own out here looking for me.

Throwing back another drink, I banish the thoughts, hellbent on escaping them for just one night. I can go back to being haunted in the morning when the hangover takes over and I'm miserable anyway.

The bar tender sweeps up the empty glass before placing another in front of me. When she sees my confusion, she nods to the pool table where I find a man looking my way. I recognize him, but I'm not sure why. I've probably seen him here before.

I raise the drink in my right hand before sucking it down greedily, adding to the growing warmth in my belly. I'm starting to feel the alcohol now, slowly numbing my racing mind.

The stranger slides onto the empty stool beside me, putting a friendly hand on my shoulder. "Hey, there," he says as he settles in, flagging the bartender.

"How's it going?" I ask, though I'm not at all in the mood for conversation.

"Oh, ya know. Living the dream," he says easily enough.

"Thanks for the drink," I offer. "But do I know you?"

"Probably not. I know you though. Heard all about you," he says, causing a red flag to wave around in my head.

"Oh really? Who are you, if you don't mind me asking?" As quick as the words pass my lips, realization hits and I know exactly who is sitting beside me, pretending to be a newfound friend.

"You're catching on, buddy. Nice to see you're not a complete idiot, even if you are fucking my old lady," he chides, the arrogance spilling from his lips.

"Wait, what?" I question, taken aback by the accusation.

"Listen, I'm not stupid. I get it. She's hot. She's also off limits, so I suggest staying away from her. Got it?"

"What the hell are you even talking about? Jade? We're just friends," I stammer, though it sounds ridiculous, even to my own ears.

"I'm not trying to cause an issue here, buddy. I just wanted to introduce myself and meet the newest man in her life, that's all. I also wanted to let you know it's time for you to move on. She's coming back home where she belongs," he continues, a stupid looking smile plastered across his face. It's about as genuine as a knock off Gucci bag.

"Yeahhhhh, no offense, but I don't think she's too interested in coming back to you, man," I say honestly. It's a laughable notion from what she's told me about her past.

"You've got it all wrong here. She's coming back home to me. I'll have her begging me to take her back, especially now that her best friend isn't around," he concludes, confidence oozing from every pore. It's sickening how delusional he is.

"Alright, whatever," I concede. I just want this interaction to be over at this point. Whatever I need to say to get him to shut up and go back to his pool game.

"That's what I thought. You're a smart man. Don't wanna end up like Emily with your throat cut in the middle of the woods somewhere," he says threateningly, holding my gaze long enough to make sure his words snake past my alcohol haze.

Once he's made it back to his game, I flag the bartender down and pay my tab. I'd rather be in my slowly enclosing apartment than stuck in this bar with him for another minute.

Chapter Twelve

Jade

The majority of the day is spent unpacking and organizing the last few boxes I picked up from Dawson's. There's a sort of finality to this step. Although the relationship is over, that was a huge chunk of my life and most of my memories in the last several years have revolved around him and Emily.

Now the memories are all I have.

I pull out a framed photo of me and Em from a trip we took with my parents sophomore year. We're standing on the beach, clad in our matching bikinis, arms thrown around each other's shoulders with blinding smiles plastered on our faces. I smile, even as the tears prick my eyes.

What I wouldn't give to go back to that time. To not know how things would turn out in the end for us.

I run my forefinger across the glass covering her face, leaving it smudged. A heaviness settles into my chest. It seems to have taken up residence there since she was killed.

The physical pain, like I can feel the strings of my heart giving way and snapping, has taken me under most nights. I don't know how to do this life without her and the days aren't getting any easier.

I've picked up on drinking, too. Terrible habit, I know. But I've found it's the only thing that soothes my soul enough to allow me to rest at all. Looking at the bottle of wine on the table, guilt starts to roll over me in waves, threatening to drown me instead of the other way around.

Scrolling back through my messages with hazy eyes, I realize I haven't heard anything new on the case in a couple days. The police have been all but absent. No new questions, no new suspects.

Thinking back to those texts I found between them, my soul splinters even further. Just when I think the hurt and betrayal is over, it finds me again, renewing my agony. I've lost everything recently. The people I cared about most are both gone from my life, leaving me empty.

As I'm falling down a rabbit hole of despair, there's a loud rasp on my door.

"Hold on!" I shout, clambering my way to my feet. I struggle to stay upright once I'm there, the alcohol in my system finally hitting me full force. "Fuck, my head," I say to myself, holding my right hand to my temple.

I make my way to the door, stumbling and nearly losing my footing over the rug in the entryway. I don't even bother to look through the peephole before yanking the door open.

When I do, I find Roman standing on the other side, shitfaced. He's every bit as plastered as I am and looking equally disturbed.

"Jade. Can I-" he starts, fumbling for his words.

I move back toward the wall, opening the door wider in invitation. "Come on in. Looks like you could use some company."

"Thanks. Appreciated," he clips, making his way toward the kitchen but not before tripping on the same corner of that stupid rug. I try to stifle the giggle that threatens to slip out, though it's really not much use. This grants me an eye roll and a middle finger, but it's also accompanied by a sexy smirk playing across his lips as his eyes devour me.

I look over him and it's like I'm seeing him for the first time. Really seeing him. He's a gorgeous man to say the least. From the wavy, jet-black hair that reaches just above his eyebrows to the stubble growing across his chin and upper lip. He's typically been clean shaven since I've met him, but I'm kinda digging this facial hair if I'm being honest. And those eyes. Dear god, I've never had any desire to drown, but I swear I feel like I could jump in and drown happily in those gorgeous ocean eyes. They have an insane intensity every time I catch him looking at me. I can feel the heat on my skin as he takes me in.

He bypasses the kitchen, then the living room, not stopping until he plops down face first onto my bed with a grunt, right after he fists the black shirt and pulls it over his head. I watch it land on the floor from the doorway, waiting for him to sit up or at least flip over onto his back. I'm damn near convinced he's passed out already when he finally lifts his head and rolls over to his back.

He lifts one hand in the air before wiggling his finger at me in a 'come here' motion. I oblige, taking the other side of the bed and lying on my back beside him, staring at the ceiling with unfocused eyes.

"Good to see I'm not the only one struggling with life tonight," he says, gesturing to the half-unpacked boxes.

"Yeah, well," I start, not wanting to make that trip back down memory lane again tonight. "Figured I might as well finish settling in here eventually."

"That's probably for the best," he agrees. "I've gotten used to having you close by." He nudges my shoulder, causing a half-smile to appear on my lips.

"It's pretty nice here," I admit. "Plus, the maintenance guy is pretty hot. You should check him out sometime." I tease, nudging him back.

"Oh yeah? I bet he's a dick," he replies. I laugh and roll my eyes.

"Nah. He's not been a dick to me at least. I can't vouch for him otherwise though," I shrug, a playful smile tugging at my mouth. The more our lighthearted banter flows, the more heat I feel between us. Each passing glance is filled with fire. Each touch creating a spark that only adds to the tension in the room.

When he runs the backs of his fingers down my arm, igniting a fire inside my veins, everything changes. His eyes are so filled with lust, but perhaps a bit more than just that. Before I can blink, he's hovering over me, mouth poised an inch from mine, waiting for my move. Or at least my permission.

With a nearly imperceptible nod, his lips crash into mine, enveloping me in a kiss that nearly drowns me in passion. His tongue presses against my lower lip, pleading for entrance. I grant it and he instantly begins exploring my mouth, like a starved man searching out a hot meal.

There's possession in his kiss, but there's an underlying ferocity in it as well. Yet it's also tender and all-consuming. By the time the contact is broken, I'm panting, eyes taking too long to refocus.

Add the insane amount of alcohol in my system to the equation and it's a recipe for disaster, but I couldn't possibly care less. I've never been kissed like that before.

I slip my hand around the back of his neck, pulling him back to me and into another soul-crushing kiss. In seconds, there are low moans between us, though I have no idea if they're coming from me or him.

I run one hand down and across his shoulder while the other tugs at his hair. He emits a low growl when I bite his lip, pulling his hair taut at the same time.

He breaks my hold, moving to pin my wrists to either side of the bed beside my head, eliciting a small whimper from me before I can stop it from escaping my lips. His weight bears down on me, pinning me in place, as he licks my skin, shoulder to the hollow of my neck, goosebumps rising in his wake.

His teeth sink into the tender flesh of my neck, forcing a gasp from my lungs. I pull against his hands, trying like hell to remove his vice-like grip so I can touch him again, but his fingers hold true, keeping me pinned beneath him. When he releases my neck, I catch the tiniest hint of a smirk at the corner of his lips.

I narrow my eyes at his enjoyment, renewing my efforts to free myself. I manage to rip one hand from his grasp and my fingernails find purchase along this shoulder blade. It's enough to welt the skin, leaving it red and angry. It's also enough to earn me a low moan from deep in his chest. Apparently, pain is his game too.

He doesn't waste time trying to recapture my wrist. Instead, his long fingers snake around my throat, squeezing the sides gently at first. The surprise must be evident in my eyes because his are nothing short of fire, becoming damn near explosive from the look on my face as realization comes over me that he is in total control here physically. I'm far from scared, though I probably should be, and do my best to rub my thighs together to ease some of the pressure that has built between them.

"A word of warning, darling. This is a game you don't truly want to get involved in. I'm not a man you should want to be with," he says, sending chills down my spine before the pressure is gone from my throat and he's off the bed entirely, snagging his shirt and heading for the living room.

"Wait! What the fuck do you mean?!" I yell, mind spinning from the sudden shift.

He takes his time to respond, still only giving me his back. "I'm just not a man you would want to be with, Jade. I don't think I'm exactly what you have pictured in your head," he explains, slipping the shirt over his head and down over his body in one smooth movement.

"That's not for you to decide! Even if I did want to be with you, it's not your place to make that decision for me," I pout, beyond confused. "And nobody said I wanted to be with you like that anyway," I continue, purely out of spite. Although, if I'm being entirely honest with myself, I've gotten used to him being around, even imagined what it would be like to be with a man like Roman.

But I'll be damned if he gets to call me out on it, especially just to tell me it's never going to happen because it isn't what I *should* want.

"I can see it, Jade," he provides, making his way toward the front door. "It was just written clearly across your face." His eyes rake my body, head to toe, then back again. He's out the front door before I can form a single word to throw back at him, leaving me standing in the living room feeling beyond stupid and utterly embarrassed.

I reach for the candle on the coffee table and throw it at the closed door, imagining it to be his back. It does nothing to ease the anger flooding my veins as the candle drops to the floor, shattering.

Leaving the problem for later, I grab the bottle of wine from the island, taking a swig before collapsing on the bed again. In the morning, I'll be beyond miserable, but that's a problem for another time.

***

When I wake midday, my first conscious thought is about my curtains. I'm pretty sure I left those open last night, too drunk to care about the consequences, whether those be peeping Toms or the sun blinding me whenever my alcohol coma allowed me to wake up. They're closed now though, leaving me puzzled.

Groaning, I roll over to the opposite side, doing my best to fight the growing nausea as my stomach churns. Between the nausea and busting headache, I'm fairly confident I would feel better if I actually *had* been hit by a bus last night.

When I'm finally able to open my eyes, I see a vase full of sunflowers on my nightstand. It's an arrangement of sunflowers and black roses, to be exact. Sitting up, I see the note laying in front of the vase. It's handwritten and messy, like it was done quickly.

Apologies will never be enough for my behavior last night. I came by this morning to check on you and try to explain. And apologize. I was out of sorts and you didn't deserve that.

I closed your curtains, hoping the sun wouldn't wake you too early. I know you're not really a rose kind of girl, but I hope you like them with the sunflowers.

If you want to talk, you know where to find me.

-Roman

I stare between the note and the flowers for several minutes before the connection really sinks in that he took time out of his morning to do this for me. Even after how last night ended up.

Forcing myself up out of bed, my feet are running for the bathroom before my brain has time to catch up. The drinks from last night are violently expelled from my body, leaving me exhausted and sore.

I opt for a long shower, throwing up a couple more times while the hot water runs over my aching body. I brush my teeth three times in the shower, scrubbing every inch of my mouth to rid it of the taste and feeling.

All the while, thoughts of Roman run rampant through my head. Memories from the beginning of our time together up until last night. I click off the water, wrapping a towel around my dripping body before heading to the kitchen for an ice water while my coffee brews.

I just can't seem to make sense of anything that happened last night. Things were perfectly fine. Then they weren't. At the thought, I glance over to see the candle has been cleaned up. Embarrassment snakes back into my bones, making me want to shrink and hide, even from myself.

As the drip from the coffee machine lulls me into a more relaxed state, a new thought hits me. How did Roman even get into my apartment this morning? I don't exactly remember locking the door, but it's a hardwired habit, I think.

I lift my foot, turning it to see the bottom. It's completely smooth and free from any cuts or traces of blood, which would have been there if I had tried to lock the door after throwing the candle. Maybe I did just leave it unlocked last night after all.

Chalking it up to a weird, drunk night full of stupid decisions, I pour the coffee and add the creamer and sugar. When the first sip hits my soul, I smile, content, as the warmth creeps out through my entire body.

I settle into the couch, laptop by my side, ready to put in a full day of writing for the first time since Emily's murder.

Chapter Thirteen

Roman

After the short trek home from Jade's apartment last night, I tossed and turned in bed for hours, replaying the night over and over. Everything had been so perfect, up until it suddenly wasn't anymore.

I had every opportunity to take things further but something just felt... off. When my hand slipped around her throat, the surprise that lit up her eyes, it was all too much. She's too innocent, even if she did seem to enjoy it as the surprise wore off.

I curse myself for not taking the time to better explain the sudden shift in my actions, but we were both drunk, though that's just another excuse for my shitty behavior.

When I heard the candle hit the door as I walked away, I knew I had made the right choice. She isn't ready for a shot at being with me. She can't handle it right now, even if she fully believes she can. And I'm not entirely sure this is what she truly wants.

I decide it's best to steer clear for a while, though my thoughts are drawn back to her throughout the night, keeping me restless. When the sun starts to rise, I slip my shoes back on and head out for some supplies, picking up some sunflowers and roses, as well as a crystal vase, in lieu of an actual verbal apology.

Knocking softly, I wait for a response. When there isn't one, I try the handle, finding it unlocked. *I'll have to remember to chastise her about that when she's in a better mood and doesn't hate me quite so much*, I think.

Letting myself in, I hear and feel the crunch of glass against the tiled floor. Sighing in frustration, I head for the kitchen, placing the vase on the counter before finding a broom and garbage can. As I bend to start sweeping the broken glass, all I can picture are the shards her heart must be in with everything she's been handling lately.

There's a heaviness in the pit of my stomach when I think about how she's hurting right now, desperate for a way to ease that pain, even for a moment. And I royally fucked it up last night.

All my recently discovered feelings for her bubble to the surface, causing the backs of my eyes to sting with unshed tears. I'm equal parts frustrated and devastated that I ruined things with her last night, seeing as I knew damn near instantly that she was it for me.

Instead of rushing to her, waking her, and trying to explain my side and why I said what I did, I clean the apartment, putting things back in place to keep her from doing it while nursing the nasty hangover she's about to endure.

I tread lightly into her bedroom, finding her passed out on the bed, still uncovered, with a bottle of wine in her hand, phone on the floor. Plugging her phone into the charger, I place the vase on the nightstand before walking to the other side of the room and closing the curtains tight. It's barely morning, but the sun will be peeking through them in no time, no doubt waking her earlier than she needs.

I gently take the wine bottle before heading to the kitchen to place it back in the fridge. I can't find the screw on cap to save my life, but maybe she will find it when she finally wakes up.

I'm halfway to the door before I turn around and head back into the apartment. I find a piece of paper and pen in the kitchen, next to her laptop. I scrawl out a quick apology note before placing it next to the vase in her bedroom.

"Ball is in your court, sunshine," I say quietly before slipping out of the bedroom, then out the front door and back to my apartment.

My phone buzzes in my pocket as I step back through the apartment door. A sinking feeling hits my stomach, the dread knocking the breath out of me. Opening the screen, I see what I've been trying to avoid has caught up with me.

Update. Now.

I stare at the message as my stomach churns and my heartrate picks up. James is not a man you want to cross, and I've been avoiding him since I saw Jade in the gym that day. I knew the time would come, but I was hoping to put it off a little longer.

There's been a slight issue. Assessing the situation currently.

I shoot off the text, lock the phone, and shut my eyes tight, rubbing the bridge of my nose with my thumb and first finger. Fuck. This isn't good.

Within seconds, the burner is vibrating in my hand. I hold my breath for a few seconds before quickly exhaling, trying to alleviate some of the stress before I get my ass handed to me.

"Yes?" I answer, trying to keep the annoyance and frustration out of my voice.

"What do you mean 'there's been an issue', Roman?" James questions, getting straight to the point. He's never been a 'how's the weather' kinda guy. Small talk just isn't his cup of tea, and I respect that, as the feeling is mutual.

"Exactly what I said. There's been an issue. I'm assessing the situation and deciding how to proceed from here," I reiterate, enunciating the words carefully.

"I can read, Roman. What kind of issue are we talking about here? Like a you can't find her issue? Or she doesn't have plans for repayment issue?" he continues, not flustered by my response.

"More like a she's dead issue," I say, waiting for the information to sink in. The line is dead for several seconds. Long enough that I wonder if he's even still on the call or halfway here to take me out for not telling him the second I found out.

"She's dead? Well, that's just wonderful," he responds sarcastically. "What happened to her?"

"That's what I'm trying to figure out. The police aren't doing shit to figure it out, so I've been doing some digging on my own. I wanted to know if someone else put out of a hit on her for a debt or if this was something else entirely."

"Keep me posted. Drop off the face of this earth again, and I'll find you. When I do, it's not going to be a good day for you," he states, hanging up the call before I get a chance to respond.

I send a text to Sara, letting her know I'm going to need an update soon. She's been consistent with keeping me in the loop so far, but I feel like this has gotten a bit out of hand with the text and call from James. I need to get this figured out quick and decide how to continue before he makes that decision for me.

I wasn't planning on getting caught up in Jade when I took this assignment. This is the last thing I saw coming, but maybe our disagreement last night was for the best and should've been left at that. At least that would have kept her out of this and safe.

I had been going to that gym since I moved to town, but the fact that Jade also worked out there made my assignment that much easier since I needed to keep tabs on her. Literally a stalker, but it's my job. I haven't had an assignment in a couple years, so I took this one serious when it came down the line. I was hesitant to take it at first, seeing as I told him I was done with this life, but it came from James himself, as a personal favor.

He had pulled me into his dimly lit office. It's the only time I've ever seen him face to face. Before I could even get a good look at his face, I could feel the energy. Powerful. Masculine. Dominating. As my eyes fell across his face, tiny white scars and all, I felt my breath catch inside my chest. His dark eyes and hair were breathtaking, but not in a particularly good way. Like they weren't meant to be that quite that dark, that haunting. When he spoke, I was taken aback, shocked by the tone and emotion in his voice.

He told me about this girl who owed a lot of money to Cain, a rival of ours, but he had a vested interest in her. She was the daughter of an old friend and he wanted to do everything in his power to keep her safe. The assignment was to bring her in so he could discuss her situation and let her know his plan. He wanted to help her.

Unfortunately, she was murdered first before any of that could come to fruition. Now, I'm stuck with the seemingly impossible task of figuring out who the fuck did it. I've often wondered if I should just tell James what's been going on and seek his guidance on how to move forward. A pair of fresh eyes to look at the evidence I've managed to dig up so far.

But there's this gnawing feeling in my stomach that keeps me from speaking the words. I need to unearth the truth on my own. He'll know everything soon enough.

As I'm pulling out my laptop, my phone is buzzing again, pulling me from my thoughts. Sara's name is flashing across the screen, and my thumb is sliding across it to pick up the call without a second of hesitation.

"Tell me something good," I say, placing the laptop on the worn coffee table and easing onto the couch. I put the phone on speaker and lay it on the table next to the computer before sitting forward, forearms on my knees, hands steepled together. I haven't been this uncomfortable or fidgety in a long time. It's unnerving, but there's a lot on the line here, so it's understandable. At least that's what I keep telling myself.

"No such luck," she says, voice strained. "I was hoping you had something for me."

"Not really anything new," I confirm, trying to keep the disappointment out of my voice. I'm at a total loss as to how to continue from here. We have absolutely nothing to go on once that video feed cut out.

"I have a few things I'm still following up on," she says, soothing some of the burn in my chest. "I should have the video in my email in about an hour if my acquaintance is able to retrieve anything after the cut off."

A long groan escapes me, easing my annoyance slightly. Scrubbing a hand down my face, I cup my jaw and prop my elbow up on my leg. "Okay," I force past my teeth. "Thank you again. Keep me updated. I'll call if I hear anything else."

The line clicks and the silence of the apartment is deafening. My ears ring from the sudden quiet, though the thoughts running in my mind are just as loud. I've never minded the chaos, never had trouble thinking during it. It's always the quiet that gets me, when I have time with my own mind.

Currently, my mind is torturing me with endless thoughts of Jade. Thoughts of last night, how great things were, and how they suddenly changed. How my behavior must have seemed irrational and beyond aggressive, though I had my reasons.

My guilt is eating me alive as I make my way to the shower to wash away the day. As the steam builds in the bathroom, clouding the mirror, I step into the shower and feel the hot water roll over my body. Quickly, my thoughts turn to how different last night could have been. She was so eager, so ready. I stopped everything because we were both beyond inebriated, though I don't think she would have denied me had we been sober. I didn't want to take her like that.

Thoughts of her kissing me while her hands roamed my body greedily has my blood flow shifting to my cock. The bastard is getting harder to ignore. It's been months since I've been with a woman, focusing on the task at hand instead. Once I saw Jade for the first time, I didn't have any real interest in other women, although I've had trouble admitting that, even to myself, until recently.

As I circle my hand around my shaft, I imagine the smooth skin of her hands around me instead. Slowly moving my hand from base to tip, I picture her on her knees before me, mouth opened, eyes eager. It doesn't take more than a minute before I'm coming undone, completely lost in the images dancing through my head.

I battle the frustration, realizing it didn't release any of the pent-up tension I had hoped to alleviate. If anything, I feel worse, more tightly wound. I turn the water to cold before forcing myself through the motions to clean my body, begging my mind to quiet. As I step out of the shower, there's a faint knock at the front door.

Wrapping a towel around my waist, I drip water through the apartment, praying to find her on the other side when I open that door.

Instead, there's no one on the other side. Just the empty parking lot. Looking in both directions, I come up empty. As I turn to go back inside, something catches my eye to my left.

It's a piece of paper, taped to my door. Pulling it off, I shut the door before opening it to find a quickly written out note.

Pick me up at 8. We can talk over dinner.

I don't even attempt to hide the smile that spreads across my face as the words sink in. I'm sure it looks goofy as hell, but if she's willing to go to dinner with me, maybe there's a shot at salvaging whatever was going on between us last night.

Thoughts of my talk with James creep in but are quickly waved away. Having dinner with Jade won't hurt anything, I decide. I'll be right back to digging for the murderer first thing tomorrow morning. For now, I head to the bedroom to get dressed.

I go for some dark washed jeans with a black Avenged Sevenfold shirt and some Vans. Putting just a touch of gel in my hair to semi-tame the dark waves, I comb through it and double check my look in the mirror. I rub my hands together to calm the nerves, but it's no use. I don't have a clue how this dinner is about to go.

After a quick pep talk, I'm out the door, letting fate take the reins for the night.

I knock on her door at eight on the dot, determined to start this date on the right foot. The door opens slowly, revealing Jade on the other side, dressed casual but cute, and I swear I've never seen a more beautiful sight.

Her hair is tucked back into a high ponytail with pieces framing each side of her face. She's gone for a very light makeup look; it makes her eyes pop beautifully. She's chosen a light blue sweater with black leggings and boots, perfect for the crisp weather tonight.

I smile as she comes into view, lightening my mood considerably. It's been rough lately, bringing out some of my less desirable qualities and moods. But just seeing her here changes that in an instant.

"You look divine," I say, the compliment slipping easily from my tongue. I try like hell to keep my eyes from ravaging her body, but it's nearly impossible. Her eyes light up, bringing a new life into her face. The tension that was in the air as she opened the door is now gone, replaced with a different tension altogether. The same one from last night, before I ruined everything.

"Thank you," she says genuinely, rubbing the elbow of one arm with the other hand sheepishly. "Same to you though."

"Why, thank you. Shall we?" I extend my arm to her and wait as she threads hers through it. "Anything specific in mind?"

"Actually, I was hoping we could go to that little old timey café down the road. If that's okay, of course." She sounds timid but hopeful.

"That sounds perfect," I say, leading us toward my Audi before opening her door and ushering her inside. The drive is quick, no more than five minutes, but the silence is strained. I have no clue what happened on the walk to the car, but the air between us is undeniably chilled suddenly. Pulling into the parking lot, I open her door before leading us inside.

"I was surprised to see the note on my door honestly," I start after we ordered drinks and entrees. "I wasn't expecting you to want to talk after last night."

"That makes two of us," she begins, making sure to lock her gaze with mine. "But I figured I deserved an explanation after the bullshit you pulled on me last night. So, here we are. Waiting for an explanation." Her hands are folded on the table, a look of impatience on her gorgeous face.

"Right. About that," I procrastinate. I was hoping to lead the date with basically any conversation other than this one. With a knot in my stomach, I continue. "I don't really have a good explanation for last night. We were both obliterated from the alcohol. I thought maybe we shouldn't push it too far and regret anything in the morning," I say honestly, even if a few key details are left out.

"Yeah, because we definitely aren't adults or anything. Absolutely couldn't make a decision like that while intoxicated and having a good time," she responds, sarcasm dripping while her eyes are rolling. "If you thought you'd regret it, you could've just led with that. I'm a big girl. I could handle it." She starts to stand but the waitress appears with our food, blocking her temporarily inside the booth.

"Thank you," I say absently. When she's left the table, I turn my attention back to Jade. "That wasn't what I meant at all and you know it. There's no way I would have ever regretted anything with you."

"I don't feel like I really know anything about you at this point, Roman. You give all the hints. All the clues are there, but any time we get close, you flip out and leave me totally bewildered. Nothing about you makes any sense." I can feel the frustration radiating off of her in waves, the fury barely beneath the surface.

"I know. I'm sorry," I state, the apology sincere. "I've been struggling lately. Inside my own head." I know the explanation sounds more like an excuse, but it's the honest to God truth about the situation. "I'm not a good man, Jade. That's the truth of it. I've done some really terrible things in the past, and there's no guarantee that I won't do more terrible things in the future. I've always had my reasons, but that doesn't make it any less grotesque."

"It should be my decision to make, Roman. You don't have the right to make that for me," she states, exasperated.

"You're right. It should have been your decision, but I was doing what I felt was right at the time. I don't want you to get involved and then end up hurt in the end. Being with me isn't easy, especially when it comes to my past." I let the silence hang in the air, allowing her time to process everything. She doesn't have a clue what she's trying to get herself into.

"Then why don't you explain it all to me? Tell me what it is that makes being with you so fucking difficult. Why can't I handle it? Why do you get to make that choice for me?" Her voice is rising, shaking with every word now. If looks could kill, I'm pretty confident I'd be making my way into the afterlife right about now.

"This isn't something I can really discuss, Jade. Remember when I said you'd just have to trust me? Well, this is what I was meaning. You just have to trust me here. The people I worked for are not all good people. They're heartless. Vile. Ruthless." I reach across the table, using a finger to turn her chin slightly so I can make eye contact. It's imperative that she sees how serious this really is. Getting mixed up with me could easily be a life or death situation for her if anything ever went wrong.

Within seconds, she breaks the contact, picking at her food absentmindedly. Anything to avoid having to face the reality sitting before her.

My phone is vibrating in my pocket, drawing my attention away from her. Sara's name is flashing across the screen, but I choose to ignore it for now, wanting to continue this conversation. Hitting ignore, I place my phone on the table before taking one of her hands in mine.

"Talk to me," I prod gently. "Tell me how you're feeling right now."

"Frustrated. As fuck. I don't understand any of what you're telling me, which is next to nothing. I don't even know you. How am I supposed to trust you on something like that?

"Also," she continues. "Why in God's name do I even care? Like I just said. I don't even really know you. I shouldn't care if you say we shouldn't be together. Nothing has happened between us at all. But, I do know there's some sort of chemistry here. Something keeps drawing me back into you, regardless of how many times it gets shut down. It's cliché as hell, but I've never felt like that about somebody before and I'm determined to figure it out." The look on her face makes it absolutely clear that she has no intention of giving in and letting this go easily.

My phone buzzes again, but this time with a text instead.

We need to talk. ASAP.

"I'm so sorry. I really need to make a phone call. I've got something that needs to be taken care of immediately. Can I see you later tonight?" I ask, my stomach suddenly churning as a sour feeling settles in deep inside me.

"You're ditching me on our date?! What the fuck, Roman. I thought we might actually have a real shot at working something out here. Seeing if there is something real between us. But I was obviously fucking delusional. Fuck off," she says, standing from the table and rushing for the front door of the café.

Fuck.

I leave a hundred on the table to cover the bill and shrug on my jacket before making my way to the door as well. Once outside on the street, Jade is nowhere to be found, of course. I definitely blew it this time, but maybe it's for the best anyway, I think for the second time recently.

"Fucking hell," I mutter to myself, frustrated beyond belief. I hit dial, wondering what's so urgent and hoping it was worth ruining any chance I had with Jade. After an eternity, she picks up the call.

"We need to meet. Now. I need you to see this," she says, diving right in. She sounds spooked to say the least. "Where is your apartment? I'm not doing this in public."

I quickly give her the address, sliding into the driver's seat and starting the car. As I pull out into traffic, I can't help the uneasy feeling that settles over me. I haven't heard Sara sound quite like that before. Something is really getting under her skin, but she doesn't seem the type to be easily rattled.

I barely remember the drive home, focused intently on getting here as fast as possible. It's only a minute or two before I hear a knock at the door. Once inside, Sara makes herself comfortable at the island, spreading out her laptop, phone, and notebook. She flips it open to a page with haphazard information doodled across it.

"Listen," she begins. "I need to know everything you know about this Jade girl. She's the one you're trying to help, right?"

"Yeah. Emily was her best friend from childhood. Murdered in cold blood a few weeks ago. I just want to help her figure out who did it," I explain, glossing over all the fine details. We've been over everything nearly a million times at this point. She knows the information inside and out.

"And you don't think she would have any motivation to do it herself?" The question lingers between us, awkward and uncomfortable.

"I mean, no, I don't think so. Jade found texts between Emily and her ex-boyfriend, Dawson, but I don't think that would cause her to murder her best friend. She seems too level headed for that," I say honestly. It had never even crossed my mind as a possibility or something to check into.

"People have murdered for less," she says, shrugging. "I got the coroner's preliminary report back today. I also got the video back from my buddy. I want you to check it out and see what you think." I nod as she's pulling up the footage on her laptop.

There's nothing going on in it for the first seven minutes, but then someone walks into the frame. Nothing stands out as they walk across the parking lot and onto the trail that leads to the popular overlook. The footage makes it hard to tell, but it does appear to be a woman, judging by the height and body shape, but she has on a hoodie with the hood up, making it impossible to pick out any further features.

Several minutes tick by with nothing happening. A few cars come and go from the parking lot. People getting out and looking around, heading to the overlook and quickly returning to their vehicles to leave.

After 18 uneventful minutes tick by, the woman from the start of the video comes back into the frame. At first, everything seems normal, but then it hits me. She walked out of the trail leading to the overlook where Emily was found, not the trail she was seen on earlier.

Her actions seem frazzled now, head moving quickly from side to side as she scans the area for other people before taking off at decent jog, heading out of the park and out of the video.

"Who the fuck was that?" I question, gesturing for her to rewind the footage. "Can you zoom in or anything? Was he able to get a clear shot of the face or anything distinguishing?" I feel the goosebumps rising across my skin, covering me from head to foot as I wait for what feels like an eternity.

"Yeah. Hold on," she says, exiting off the video and pulling up some fairly grainy photos. They've been enhanced enough to make out some decent features. As she clicks through the pictures, ice fills my veins. She flips through them slowly, taking in my reaction and the moment it hits me.

My stomach churns, threatening to spill the contents from my date with her earlier tonight. I feel the color drain from my face as I stare at the images, shocked to my core.

It's only when Sara clicks the last photo that the reality of the situation hits me full force.

"Is that…" I start, unable to form the words around the lump in my throat. With every picture, I'm more certain. It's Jade on the screen. "Oh god. There's no way. That can't be right." I stare at the screen, mind racing.

"I wasn't completely sure, Roman. This is the best he was able to do without distorting the images a ton," she says, placing her hand on my arm in an awkward attempt at comfort. "That's why I wanted to show you these pictures and rehash what you knew about her, if she was even capable of doing this. I also have the coroner's report." She pauses, waiting for my brain to catch up. It takes several seconds before I'm able to form a coherent thought.

"Fuck," I start, pausing as my brain struggles to catch up. "Yeah. Yeah, let's look at it. What does it say?" I feel like the world is spinning faster or something, like a whirlpool threatening to suck me under.

She pulls up the report easily before turning the screen toward me. She's already read it by now. Judging by her actions, I'm assuming the worst at this point.

Decedent: St. John, Emily, Rose

Race: White   Sex: Female   Age: 24

**Requested by Haven County Police Department*

Eyes: Hazel   Hair: Brown

Weight: 147.2lbs   Height: 5'4"

Marks and wounds: scrapes and cuts to both hands, bruise on right cheekbone – black eye, scrapes on both knees and lower legs, abrasions to back of head, bruises with clear finger shapes on neck. Most scrapes are superficial in natural, indicative of defensive wounds.

Probable cause of death: Asphyxiation with blunt force trauma to the head

Manner of death: homicide

My mind goes blank, nearing total shut down. "This is the coroner's report? For Emily? And that was Jade. Walking out of the park. Where Emily died. Oh, my god."

Fucking hell. There's no way Dawson killed Emily. At the bar, he mentioned ending up with my throat cut, just like Emily. Nothing he said that night lines up with what the coroner's report states.

"Hold on. There's more," Sara says sheepishly. "I was able to track their phone locations from that night. They were both pinging off the same tower while Jade was at the park, meaning Emily was still there. She never left from the time we saw her there with Dawson. He left alone."

Chapter Fourteen

After my meeting with Sara last night, I full on crashed. She left around ten, and I hardly remember anything that happened after that.

I know I showered, shaved my face, and tried to get some work done, but my head just wasn't in it. I couldn't concentrate, given everything that transpired during the night.

Opening my phone, I see several texts and a couple missed calls from Jade.

Clicking the thread of messages, I realize I texted her at some point, saying we needed to talk, which then sent her into a fit of rage, judging by the messages throughout the night. The longer they went unanswered, the angrier she became from the looks of it.

The frustration is a hair's breadth from boiling over right now. Slipping on some shoes, I head to the gym to work out some of my stress before getting back with her later. It's only going to explode if I try to talk to her right now. One of us has got to be level-headed, and it sure as fuck isn't going to be her apparently.

As I make my way to the gym, memories come flooding in. Memories from the first time I saw her here. How it was just an assignment. I needed to infiltrate Emily's life somehow, and the best way I've found to do that is by getting close with someone your target already trusts.

Typing in my code on the lock, I glance through the front window, eyes landing on the one person I'm determined to avoid right now. Jade. Fucking hell.

She's red-faced, sweaty, and insanely angry. Looks like great minds think alike. She looks like she's on a war path, and I'm not ready to face that problem just yet.

Thinking better of it, I turn back toward the street, opting for a run instead. Being in the gym with her is a recipe for disaster.

"What the fuck?!" About a mile into my run, something slams into the back of my head. Turning halfway, I see the water bottle rolling slowly across the road toward the grass. Ripping my earbuds out, I whirl around, finding Jade directly behind me. And she's furious. I swear if this was a cartoon, she'd have steam coming out of her ears.

"What the actual fuck?" I yell, stepping away from her to create some space. "What's your problem?" *My* problem is that she's absolutely breathtaking, even engulfed in rage. Somehow it brings a mesmerizing light to her eyes, making it damn near impossible to look away, even when I know I should.

"MY problem?! Oh, I don't know, Roman," she yells back, lifting her hand to tick off each offense. "Maybe the fact that you *ditched* me on our date last night! Or that you texted me saying we needed to talk and then fucking ignored me the entire night! Maybe that you're man enough to come to the gym but too chicken shit to come inside because I was there working out!" She puts her hands on her hips, fury radiating from her.

"Did you think that maybe I got lost in my own head last night and didn't even realize I didn't text you back? Or maybe I wasn't ready to see you this morning because I had shit to work out for myself first so that's why I didn't come in the gym? Or perhaps something came up last night and I didn't actually *want* to leave our date but I didn't really have a fucking choice?" I let the questions hang between us for a few seconds before finishing. "Of course not because that would mean it was about someone other than Jade."

As the words hit home, her face morphs into one of both shock and rage, as well as pain. Maybe even a little embarrassment.

I spin back around and start jogging, determined to be as far away from her as possible. All I can think about when looking into her eyes now is how she murdered her best friend. How she cried to me about it, hellbent on finding out who took Emily's life when the killer was in front of me the entire time.

Within feet, I'm bent over, puking up the little bit of breakfast I was able to choke down this morning.

I'm in love with a killer.

It takes less than a second for my brain to shift, trying to make an excuse for all of the evidence pointing to her being the murderer.

Maybe she had a good reason. It's not like I know the whole story at this point. I'm just making assumptions. It's easy to assume it was because of Emily and Dawson, but maybe it was self-defense. Yeah, that has to be it. My brain grasps at straws, latching onto anything that keeps me from having to let her go.

Before I'm able to spin even more out of control, she's beside me, rubbing my back to soothe me. The thoughts go silent, as if they were never there to begin with. That's the scary thing about whatever this is with Jade. She's able to calm the storm inside me just by being around.

"I really need some time alone," I say, sitting and pulling my knees to my chest. The last thing I want is for her to leave, but it's exactly what I need right now. I can't think when she's around.

Silence envelops us for several seconds before she responds. "Okay," she starts. "I'll go. You know where to find me when you get whatever the fuck this is sorted out."

She stands with shaky legs, looking as if it takes every ounce of will she has left to leave me here. She knows I'm fighting a losing battle, even if she doesn't know what it's about. She's willing to fight these demons with me without questioning it, but in the end, my request wins out and she starts the trek back to town on her own, not bothering to look back.

Gathering every drop of energy I have left, I stand and start making my way to the overlook. I'm not sure why, but being there feels like the right place to be while I try to sort all of this out.

In 15 minutes, I'm leaning against the old metal railing, looking out at the river below. For the first time, my mind is entirely quiet. No matter how much I try to think about the situation at hand, my mind remains silent, as if there's really not anything to think about at all.

Everything feels... final. Like there's nothing else to be done now, other than have this conversation with Jade and move on with my life.

With a deep sigh, the heavy feeling filters in, weighing me down again. I drag my feet along the path, making my way back to my apartment.

Chapter Fifteen

Jade

"What the fuck?!" Staring down at Dawson's phone, text messages pulled up, everything starts to go fuzzy. The texts are from Emily. My best friend.

It doesn't take more than a minute to put the pieces together. Scrolling back, I realize this has been going on for longer than I could've imagined. Weeks of betrayal from both sides, the people I trusted the most holding the knife that has now been firmly planted into my back.

As I read on, my stomach begins to churn, taking in the full scope of their relationship. The texts paint a vivid scene of their life together, along with the plans for a future once I'm 'out of the way', as they've so kindly put it.

Dawson: Em, we can't do that. She's not a part of this.

Emily: What else do you expect me to do?! There's not another way out of this mess, D. You know that as well as I do.

Dawson: I guess you shouldn't have gotten yourself into this fucked up situation then, huh? It's not right for Jade to pay for your fuck up. Figure it out.

Mess? What kind of mess is Emily in? And how does it have anything to do with me? Panic starts to set in at the tone of their texts. Concern for my longtime friend seems to trump everything I just learned about her deception for the moment.

My mind is spinning, faster and faster until I'm physically dizzy, which spurs the nausea. Thoughts of how I missed all the clues, the time we've all spent together, and all the memories rush to the forefront of my mind, and for just a moment, I'm crushed. The sadness creates a physical ache inside my chest that I would imagine being akin to being squeezed to death by a giant vice of some sort. It's a pain unlike anything I've ever encountered before.

The boiling rage surfaces shortly after, pulling me from the bed we've shared for so long. Suddenly desperate to be as far from him as possible, I make my way to the kitchen silently, thoughts swirling of the future and what comes next.

As I shut the fridge door, lo and behold, Emily appears out of thin air on the far side of the kitchen, rubbing her eyes to clear the sleep. I didn't hear her come in, but I was also intently focused on my next move, trying my best to shut out the outside world.

After handing her a quick cup of coffee, attempting to keep my composure until I can make a solid plan, I head back to the bedroom to take a shower so I can start my day. Moping around isn't going to help anything here.

The hot shower helped tremendously to clear my head, letting me see things for what they actually are, even though I don't have all the pieces yet.

I spend the next couple hours at the gym, pushing myself beyond exhaustion so that my mind will quiet.

I make my way to my favorite spot in the entire world after leaving the gym. Even though my legs feel like jelly, I force them to carry me to the overlook, desperate for the calm it will bring to my soul.

When the air takes on a chill, I resign myself to the facts. I threw my phone out into the river, determined to have this time to myself after finding out that my high school sweetheart has been cheating on me with my childhood best friend. They had been blowing up my phone, so the split-second decision seemed like the only real option at the time. Now it's time to head home and handle the mess. Unfortunately.

I make my way down the path, doing my best to carefully step over the bigger rocks, which isn't super easy considering I don't have much light at this point.

A snapping twig sends me into an immediate panic. Heartrate spiking, adrenaline coursing through my veins, I beg my tired legs to carry me down the path and back to safety before whatever boogeyman is in the woods has a chance to drag me back inside.

Making it back to the parking lot, I hit my knees, gasping for breath, partly from the fear but partly from the adrenaline and everything that has happened today. Rolling my eyes, I force myself slowly back to my feet and make my way home.

It takes nearly an hour to make the short trek home. I drag my feet, dreading the interaction altogether. I still don't know what to do, but I do know this has to be faced. There's really no moving forward without it.

Walking through the front door, I wonder if the house is empty. There's not a single sound, no lights on, no movement. Just as I'm exhaling a sigh of relief, Dawson appears from the kitchen, looking worn and worried.

"Fuck," he says, voice breathy. The instant change in his demeanor would be heartwarming any other time. He instantly relaxes as I come into his view. "I've been so worried about you, Jade. Where have you been? I've tried to call and texted you a dozen times." The words rush out of his mouth as if he can't quite say them fast enough.

Ignoring him entirely, I push past him into the kitchen. Grabbing a cup, I fill it with ice and water before heading for the living room. I can feel the vice again, squeezing the air out of my lungs. I've never been good at this kind of thing.

"We need to talk," I start, placing the glass on the wooden coffee table and settling into the leather couch.

His face pales instantly as he makes his way to the chair opposite me and sinks into it. All the happiness and hope that was so evident in his features before are washed away and replaced by despair.

"About what?" he asks, feigning ignorance. The look in his eyes gives him away. He's been waiting for this to come about.

"I think you probably know," I say, letting the accusation hang in the air between us. It's tense to say the least. "Where's Emily?" I ask, finishing off this dance we've had going on. There's no doubt what I want to discuss now.

"Fuck," he murmurs, scrubbing his hand down his face in frustration. "Fuck, fuck, fuck." His eyes are bouncing between anger and desperation. He doesn't know how to feel just yet, waiting to see my full reaction.

"I saw the texts," I state, giving him nothing further. Leaning back into the couch, I squirm in an attempt to get more comfortable, though the discomfort is anything but physical.

"Jade, you've gotta understand. It wasn't what it looked like. Not exactly anyway. I know everybody says that and it's so damn cliché. But it's the truth," he starts, words rushing out as quick as his mouth can move.

"Yes, I cheated on you. We've been seeing each other for a little while now. Probably three or four months I guess. It was wrong and shouldn't have ever happened, but it did. There's a way bigger issue though. I ended things with Emily when I found out what her actual intentions were, Jade," he pleads, begging me to understand.

"And what were those, Dawson? To be with your forever, push me out of the picture, take my place with you?" I ask sarcastically, fully knowing the answer to my questions.

"No. Not at all. Well, I mean, yeah, that was part of it. But this is so much more than that. You're at risk, Jade. You're not safe. Once I figured that out, I told Emily we were done, but I couldn't just ignore her entirely or you would've known something was up. I can't stand to even look at her anymore," he explains, paling to a point I didn't even know was possible.

"What could've possibly been so terrible, Dawson? Sooo much worse than exiling her best friend and destroying her relationship? Doesn't really get much worse than that I don't think."

"Oh, you'd be so surprised. It gets so much worse than that," he states, locking his gaze with mine. "You're never going to believe me when I tell you what she said to me. But I swear to you on everything holy that it's the truth. I don't have any solid proof since I deleted everything she sent in text and a lot of it was said in person."

I wait for him to go on, already refuting the words that haven't even come out of his mouth. He's lied about everything else. How am I supposed to believe anything he says now? For all I know, Emily decided she didn't want to be with him after all, so he's playing her to be the bad guy here so he can look slightly better in the end.

He pulls in a deep steadying breath before blowing it out in a quick exhale. Threading his fingers together, he locks eyes with me again. "You're not safe, Jade. Em got into some trouble a while back. She's had a problem for a while that we had no idea about. She got mixed up with some bad people and owes them a ton of money that she can't pay back." He pauses, giving me enough time to process the words before continuing.

"She told me she started gambling back in high school. Just small stuff at first. Scratch off tickets, pull tabs, that kind of stuff. It got worse as time went on and she started losing quite a bit of money. She traded favors for payment for about a year. Sexual favors. To all these nasty men who had a hold on her because she fucked up and got addicted to the high of winning. One thing led to another and she eventually got in way too deep.”

“Okay? That sounds like her problem?” I volley back, hellbent on not feeling any sympathy for her at this point. She made her bed. Now she has to lie in it.

“I fully agree with you,” he starts again, hesitation clear in his posture now. “But there’s where Em and I disagreed apparently. Instead of just coming to either of us for help, she tried to battle this beast on her own and lost. She was desperate for a way out, to start her life over without having to look over her shoulder constantly. So, in the end, she offered you up to them as payment.” He flinches as the gravity of the situation hits me dead center in the chest.

“She what?!” I yell, losing my composure entirely. “You’re lying to me right now. Emily’s capable of a lot of shady shit, but she would never do that. Never. I know her better than that.” Even as I deny the information, a sinking feeling takes root in my stomach. In my heart of hearts, I know he’s telling the truth.

“I’m so sorry, Jade. I had no idea. As soon as I found out, I ended things with her, but I had no clue how to tell you without admitting to everything that has been going on and I wasn’t ready to face the end of what we had.” The grief in his eyes is almost heartbreaking. The man has lost everything. “I just wanted to keep you safe. That was the most important thing. I begged her not to go through with it. She said she wouldn't, but I have no way of knowing if she was telling the truth or not. I don't know how to protect you," he admits, the anguish finally taking over as the first tears spill from his red-rimmed eyes.

For the first time in quite a while, I really take him in. Really look at his face, the small wrinkles around the corners of his mouth from all the smiles and laughs during our years together. It truly does sadden me to realize our time together has come to an end and there will be no more memories to make.

However, I know my place now. And if what he says is true, I'm in more danger than I've ever been in before. Taking in a shaky breath, I pull myself together enough to get up and walk out of the living room, down the hall, and out the front door.

By late evening, I've managed absolutely nothing aside from wallowing in self-pity, wondering how my life has gotten to this point and where I'm supposed to go from here.

With no conscious thought, I eventually find myself walking into the park again. Somehow, I keep getting drawn here, back to this place I used to find safe.

I notice a silver car with rental plates on the back as I walk toward the trail to the main overlook. *Weird,* I think to myself before making my way to the edge of the overlook, losing myself to the rampant thoughts for only God knows how long.

Heading back toward the parking lot, I contemplate the next steps I need to take. I have nowhere to go, nothing to my name at this point. Also, I happen to be starving. I can't even remember the last time I ate at this point.

Feet scrubbing along the dirt path, I freeze, hairs standing up along the back of my neck, suddenly alert. Within seconds, Emily comes into view on the trail, between me and the parking lot.

"Jade! My god, I've been looking everywhere for you!" she exclaims, taking a step toward me. When I take a step back away from her, she pauses, confusion painting her beautiful face. "Jade? What the fuck?"

"Why are you here, Em?" I question, accusation clear in my eyes. I don't want to be anywhere near her. I just wanted some space to breathe and think through everything. Not come face to face with my current nightmare.

The next instant, I'm walking down the trail back toward the parking lot. Except it isn't the well-worn trail to the popular overlook I was just on. I'm walking down the small, mostly overgrown trail that leads to my favorite view of the river.

Gasping for air, clutching my chest, I sit straight up in my bed. The fear running through my veins is palpable, leaving my skin coated in goosebumps and sweat.

I can't remember anything that happened between seeing Emily on the trail in front of me and walking out of the overgrown path back into the parking lot. It's all a blur.

It takes nearly a minute to calm my rapid breaths and slow my heart rate. I can still feel it beating against my rib cage, making a futile – yet honorable – attempt at escape.

It's still the middle of the night, judging by the darkness outside my apartment window. Holding my hands against my temples, I take a deep ragged breath, willing myself to calm down.

It was just a nightmare, I tell myself, chest still wound tight. Just a nightmare.

Chapter Sixteen

Roman

After making my way back to the apartment last night, I zoned out completely. All I really remember is staring at the wall, blank, for what seemed like hours. Nothing spinning through my head, no torturous thoughts to antagonize me. Just... nothing.

The emptiness was damn near too much to bear. I went from feeling completely carefree and happy every moment I spent with her to feeling numb and empty, a feeling I've spent way too many years getting comfortable with.

Except this time is different. This time, there's an undeniable loss attached to that emptiness. An ache that is so much more than skin deep.

Fighting the feeling was futile, given all the circumstances surrounding it, so I finally caved, crawling into my bed to let the silence engulf me entirely.

Waking early this morning after a night of more tossing and turning than actually sleeping, I stretched my sore muscles, not at all ready to take on whatever bullshit the world had in store for me today.

Thinking back on the last 24 hours, I huff quietly as I force myself from the slight comfort of my bed, feeling mentally and physically drained. The night of no real rest didn't do me any favors, nor did it help my mood for the day.

I've been debating on the best way to handle the situation with Jade, but so far, I'm coming up short. There's no good answer here. Either way this goes, I don't see a positive outcome for anybody honestly. And the last thing I want to do is lose the one safe place I've managed to find in this fucked up world.

Changing into some sweatpants and a loose t-shirt, I slip on some shoes, desperate to find some breathing room. The hope of fresh air brightening the mood is quickly doused with a crack of lightning, followed by a distant rumble of thunder.

Great, I think. *Exactly what I needed today.* However, when the first heavy raindrops fall a few minutes later, I don't seek shelter away from the storm. Instead, I let it swallow me whole, consuming me. It's uncomfortable at first. Annoying truthfully. But soon, I notice my worries and anxieties seem to be washing away with the water running down my body.

As if the rain is cleansing more than just my body, washing away any remnants of the bad mood I've been in since I saw that video, I feel my spirit lighten a bit. For just a moment, I can breathe deeply and believe that everything is going to work out in the end. That's what everyone always says, isn't it?

Once I'm thoroughly soaked, I realize there's a big goofy ass smile plastered across my face. With drops of water falling from my lashes and the tip of my nose, I relish the feeling while it lasts, laughing like a lunatic.

Sometimes, a rainy day is exactly what you need to get your head on straight.

***

"I think we probably need to talk," I begin, heart pounding frantically in my chest, desperate to end this conversation before it even begins. *It's necessary,* I remind myself, refusing to give in to the desire to smooth everything over and avoid this all together.

"Honestly, I don't know if there's even anything to talk about, Roman," she says, leaning against the frame of her front door.

Once the high of the rain had faded away, leaving me feeling cold and empty once again, I headed to my apartment for some dry clothes before making my way to Jade's apartment, determined to finish this once and for all.

The second she opened the door, my heart faltered. She was stunning even though she was dressed casually, no makeup, with her hair in a messy bun on top of her head. The oversize black and purple tie-dyed t-shirt with black gym shorts tied the lazy day look together perfectly, leaving me breathless momentarily.

"Can I come in?" I ask, not wanting to push it too far. It's a conversation that needs to be had but pushing her right off the bat isn't going to be beneficial to anybody.

With a heavy sigh, she drops her eyes to the floor before turning to trudge to the living room, leaving the door wide open for me. Breathing a sigh composed of relief and hesitation, I step into the apartment, knowing it's the point of no return. That knowledge alone makes me want to puke.

I sit on the edge of the leather couch as she fills two glasses with water in the kitchen before joining me. The ice clinks as she sets them on the coffee table coasters before taking the seat opposite me.

She pulls her knees up toward her chest before leaning back into the chair to get more comfortable. "So," she says, refusing to let the awkward silence continue any longer.

"I just think there's a lot to talk about here. I'm conflicted about everything that's going on and I really need some clarity," I start, not wanting to accuse her of anything without getting her side of the story.

"Same though. I don't know what's going on between us, if anything, so some clarity there would be nice," she agrees.

"Um, we can absolutely talk about that. But I wanted to talk to you about something else first," I say, wringing my hands between my knees in front of me. I can't bring myself to look at her, knowing she will lock eyes with me and my resolve will instantly crumble. This woman is the embodiment of kryptonite.

"Okay?" she says, cocking her eyebrow, confusion written across her face. "What did you wanna talk about then? I thought we were on the same page here."

I chance a glance at her, taking in every tiny detail about her. I do my best to memorize it all in case this is the end of my time with her, yet hoping there's some sense of salvation to be found in her response to the impending questions.

"We are. Well kinda. I do want to talk about that. But I think there's a more pressing issue that needs to be discussed beforehand." I'm stalling. The anxiety building in my body is making me physically uncomfortable, like I might explode at any second.

"I don't know how to even bring any of this up, Jade," I say, wringing my hands again, trying to figure out the right words to say but coming up with nothing. After just a second of hesitation, I plunge into the deep end before I lose the balls to say anything at all.

"You told me that Emily was murdered right after we first met. That first drunk night we spent together. I spent the entire night feeling sick over how upset and hurt you were, pledging to myself that I would get to the bottom of the situation, or at least try to," I explain, letting the words spill from the bottom of my soul without restriction.

Her face is calm and composed, but her eyes are wild and frantic, wondering where all of this is heading, no doubt. The energy shift in the room is tangible, from sadness and confusion to an intense fear. From both sides it seems.

"I was able to get into contact with some people who helped me piece everything together, at least somewhat. We got access to the coroner's report, as well as some surveillance footage from the parking lot at the overlook," I pause, waiting for that information to sink in. The look in her eyes shifts as it does. She knows I know.

"I saw you, Jade. I saw Emily arrive at the park with Dawson. I saw you walking up the path to the other overlook shortly after they arrived. After a while, 18 minutes to be exact, you walked back to the parking lot, but not from that same path, right? You came from the other side, the overgrown path. The same path where Emily was found early that next morning." I let everything out, deciding it's best to just lay everything out on the table, in the open.

I wait, giving her space to collect herself and decide how we're going to proceed from here. It takes several minutes before she says anything at all.

She wipes a lone tear sliding down her cheek before finding her voice. "It's not what it seems, Roman," she begins, voice shaky. "Okay, it actually is exactly what it seems. Or at least I think it is. Fuck, I don't even know anymore," she voices, sounding a little more confident now.

I lean back into the soft leather, not putting any pressure on her to continue until she's ready. I'm doing my very best to keep an open mind about what she has to say, even though the case seems open and shut to me. In all my years of collection work, rarely was any situation other than what it seemed.

"God, I think I did kill her." With that admission, and I'm assuming the first time she voiced it out loud, she springs up from her chair and sprints to the kitchen before violently expelling the contents of her stomach into the trash can.

Once the dry heaves subside, she rests her head on her forearm, still poised over the can just in case. "Fuck. I killed my best fucking friend," she says, just above a whisper. "I don't even remember any of it. Hand to God, I don't remember anything past when she found me on the trail that night. The next thing I remember clearly was walking out of the overgrown trail and back into that parking lot. I remember feeling sick, like there was poison or something pumping through my veins. Something just felt wrong." She lifts her head to look at me, sincerity burning bright in her eyes.

"What happened, Jade?" I ask, keeping my voice calm, refusing to let any negative tone creep in. I want answers. None of this makes any sense. Jade isn't the type to just kill her best friend, even if that friend was cheating with her boyfriend.

"I read the messages. Jesus, those messages. They were brutal," she recalls, pain seeping into her features from the memory. "They were together. For way longer than I could have ever expected. I never saw any of the signs, but it's all so clear looking back." For a minute, she pauses, lost in the memory.

"Anyway," she continues, making her way back to the chair on shaky legs. "I was pissed. Honestly, that doesn't even begin to scratch the surface of what I was feeling. But I just wanted out. Killing either of them never even crossed my mind. I just wanted to get my stuff and start over, focus on myself and building a life where neither of them existed."

"So what happened? Something changed," I prod.

"I kept reading," she says with a small shrug. "Which was followed by a conversation with Dawson where he told me everything. Things that shook me and changed the way I viewed the most important people in my life." With some hesitation, she continues.

"You're not going to believe me though. Everything I found out from Dawson was insane. Hell, I didn't believe it myself at first." She peers at me, sheepish and red-faced from the tears.

"Try me," I say, fully invested.

She pulls in a full breath, inflating her entire chest, before blowing it out in a rush. "Emily wasn't at all who I thought she was. At least not for the last few years," she explains, locking her gaze with mine. "She got into a lot of trouble, according to Dawson. She started gambling a few years ago, which turned into a huge problem fairly quickly. She got in with some bad people and owed them more money than she could have ever reasonably expected to pay back."

Swallowing the emotion, she bats at her eyes again, though new tears instantly replace the ones she swiped away.

"She traded her body to repay the debt. Or at least some of it. But she was in too far for that to satisfy these disgusting men," she says, a grimace contorting her features. "She was trying so hard to get out of that world, but nothing she did seemed to make a difference. She never even told me. Never came to me for any help at all. I never had a clue." She drops her eyes to the floor, shaking her head in disbelief.

"There's no way you could have known, Jade," I soothe, desperate to ease her pain even as my own head spins.

"People are good at hiding things. Especially those kinds of things. They don't want us to see the darkest parts of them, no matter how close we are."

Nodding, she wipes away more tears. "I know. I know there wasn't anything I could have done differently. She didn't come to me, and that isn't my fault. But the fact that she's dead *is* my fault." She pins me with her gaze before speaking again. Not once has she tried to deny what she's done, and for that, I give her props. Damn near every human on this planet would have been denying it, trying to get out of what they'd done.

"The most shocking thing of all is that my best friend in this entire world was planning to trade *me* to these men to settle her debt." The finality in her voice takes me by surprise.

I can only imagine the look of shock that filters across my face. *What? There's no way. What kind of vile person would do that?! I knew Emily was in a lot of trouble, but I didn't realize she would stoop that low.* My mind races when this last piece of the puzzle clicks into place.

Everything I knew from James corroborated Jade's story, making the new information easily believable. Why would she lie about that if she so willingly admitted the rest of the story, including her own fucked up part in it? Fuck.

"What happened at the overlook, Jade?" I question, voice firm as I try to piece together that last tidbit that remains unknown.

Pulling her eyes up to mine, I notice they're filled with a sorrow I've seldom seen. Seeing her look so lost and hurt causes an ache to grow in the pit of my stomach. The urge to go to her, to take the pain away - even for a moment - is overwhelming.

With a shaky exhale, she begins to recount the events from that night. There's a subtle strength in her voice now that wasn't there a few moments ago. She's reciting facts now, completely devoid of the emotions she felt when recalling her former best friend. Memories of the good times.

There's a shocking coldness in her tone now. "I went to the overlook to clear my head after I talked to Dawson," she starts, gaze dropping down to her hands where she picks at her fingernails absentmindedly. "I didn't know what to do or have anyone to turn to really. I knew the gym wouldn't cut it that time, so I wanted to look out over the river. Think things through, ya know?" She shrugs before wrapping her arms around her knees that are tucked against her chest again.

"I stayed there forever it seemed. Completely lost in my head. After a while, I decided to head out and try to get a plan together to move forward. I remember thinking there were so many things to do now. Pack my shit, find a place to stay... on and on. I was super overwhelmed." She pauses, lost in the memory of that night. Her eyes look far away, even from here.

"All of a sudden, I got chills. In the next second, Emily was standing in front of me, acting over the top, like she was out of her mind with worry for me." She pauses to roll her eyes dramatically. In any other situation, it would have made me laugh. "She wasn't concerned for me," she continues, looking up at me now. "She didn't give a fuck about me," she says, quieter this time, the hurt evident in her voice.

"She did care about you, Jade. She was just lost. When people get in that far, they do things you could never have imagined them doing. They're desperate for a way out, even if that means destroying everyone in their life in order to get that," I explain, thinking about all the people I've tracked down over the years. None of them were inherently bad people. They just got into some really fucked up situations and had to do some even worse things to survive.

"Yeah. Maybe," she says, brushing the thought to the side. "Anyway. I didn't want to see her then. I was pissed. As anyone would have been," she glances up, looking for confirmation, but when I don't make a move, she continues her story. "She wanted to talk. I didn't. I just wanted to get away from her, but she wasn't going to let that happen. I pulled her over toward the overgrown overlook so we could talk without other people around."

As I listen to her talk, my whole body is screaming for me to go to her. Pull her into my arms and make everything else go away. I pull my feet up onto the couch, moving my hands underneath my thighs in an attempt to calm to urge.

"I asked her about it. About everything Dawson had said. She admitted to all the shit about the gambling, about owing those pigs so much money. About selling her body to appease them temporarily. When I asked her about her plans for me, everything I've ever known about her changed. She calmly told me that yes, she had full intentions of trading me to them, knowing what they were capable of, in order to settle the score. In order to give her a chance at a happy life with *my* boyfriend." The tears are pouring in streams down her cheeks, though I'm betting they're half from heartbreak and half from rage.

"When I asked her why, she just shrugged her shoulders. Then she told me I never deserved the life I had with Dawson anyway. I was never good enough. That for years, she had remained friends with me so she could stay close with him, hoping to eventually get her shot at a life with him." This time when she looks up, there's a fire that has taken over her eyes. I've never seen someone look so terrifying, yet she remains the most beautiful woman I've ever laid eyes on.

I can feel the rage building in my chest for her. Nobody deserves to be treated that way, let alone by their best friend since childhood. If she wasn't already dead, I'd kill the bitch myself just for those comments, James and his motives be damned.

"At that point, I just kinda lost my shit," she admits, curling more into herself, though I didn't truly think that was possible. She looks so tiny, fragile even. But the rage pouring off her in waves says otherwise.

"What happened from there?" I ask, genuinely interested in how she did it. After hearing her story, I can already feel my defenses wavering. *Fuck.*

"It's all a little fuzzy to be totally honest with you. I know I killed her. I just don't remember all the details of how it happened." She takes a minute, doing her best to recall the details. Closing her eyes, tiny wrinkles appear at the edges as she squeezes them tight, focusing on every detail she can remember.

"I remember hearing her explanation. All those vile things she spewed at me. I remember the anger building up, feeling like my chest was going to explode if I didn't release it somehow." Her eyes cloud with the memory, pulling her back to that night once again. "I was shocked and hurt. Betrayed. I pushed her backward, causing her to trip over a tree root and land on the ground, hands out behind her to brace the fall. It's fucked up, but I remember thinking how weak she looked in that moment."

Can't deny that's kinda hot. My outrage at what she did has completely vanished, replaced by a feeling I can't quite place. It's almost as if I'm *proud* of her after finding out what actually happened.

"Her face was twisted with anger. I had never put my hands on her, no matter how bad the fight was. I wasn't able to contain myself that night. Once she was on the ground, she was fuming. The next few minutes are all a blur. I can't remember anything in particular really. I just know we kept hitting each other, over and over and over. I kept getting more and more angry, like every hit was stoking a fire in my blood." She stops to chance a look at me, relieved when she finds no judgement in my eyes.

"Next thing I know, I'm straddling her on the ground, hands wrapped around her throat. I picked her head up, slamming it back into the dirt beneath her several times. Five, six maybe. I remember my hands finally giving out from the effort of squeezing her throat for so long. It didn't really hit me that she was dead though, even as her glossy eyes stared up at the sky above me. Not until I rolled off of her, collapsing on the ground next to her and there was total silence. Not a single sound. That's when I knew." She suddenly looks ill, like she might throw up at any second, though she does her best to school her features and appear calm.

"Fuck," is the only response I'm capable of giving. The tears streaming down her cheeks slow before she wipes away the last of them. The weight of the spoken truth seems to lift from her, though the reality of the situation is still grim.

Chapter Seventeen

Jade

He didn't run.

That's the first coherent thought running through my mind when I finish retelling the story of that night.

I told him every horrid thing I did, all the gruesome details I could remember, and not once did he offer to run or tell me I'm a monster or threaten to go to the police.

I told him everything, and he chose to stay.

The reality of that hits me hard, knocking the air from my lungs. *There's gotta be something wrong with this guy's head,* I think.

"So that's it?" he asks, hands steepled in his lap, eyes focused on the tips of his fingers as they press together.

"Yeah. Basically," I confirm, too ashamed to even attempt to look up at him.

"Why did you cry to me that night in your apartment? Tell me all about your best friend being murdered and the cops not doing shit to find the killer? You're either a hell of an actor, or something isn't adding up here," he counters.

"Honestly? I was drunk and in complete denial," I say, determined to lay everything out on the table. He already knows what I did. There's no sense in hiding anything now. "At that point, none of the details were clear to me. I had blocked every memory as soon as it happened apparently. It wasn't until I started having the nightmares that the pieces started to click for me," I explain, shuddering at the thought of those damned nightmares. They've been haunting me almost every night since the murder.

"Nightmares?" he asks, eyebrow cocked.

"Yeah. A couple nights after all that, I started having recurring nightmares about what I did. They've gotten more clear as time goes on, but there are still fuzzy details in there."

"So that night at the apartment? It was sincere? You really didn't know who had killed her then?" he asks, sounding skeptical for the first time. Hell, I can't even blame him for that one.

"Hand to God, I didn't remember at that point. Until the dreams came, I sincerely thought Dawson had killed her.

He was acting super sketchy about everything after she was found. It made sense that he would have done it. Or at least that's what I thought then," I shrug, not knowing what else to say.

"Fuck. That's a lot to take in," he sighs, leaning back into the couch, exhaustion etched across his face.

"I'm still trying to figure it out myself," I confess. "Sometimes I want to go turn myself in, get it off my conscience. But other times," I pause, shrugging.

"I don't think anyone could blame you, given the circumstances. The bitch was trying to *sell* you for fuck's sake! If we could prove it, it's easily a case of self-defense in my opinion. Self-preservation really, I guess," he adds easily. "Anyone would have done the same if they were in your shoes, whether they'll admit to it or not."

I breathe a sigh of relief. I don't know what I had been expecting, but that wasn't it. I've spent this whole time trying to justify my actions to myself, but to have someone else put it into words is an incredible relief.

"While we're at it," he begins, "I guess it's my turn to confess." He eyes me cautiously, waiting for me to give the go ahead. When I nod slightly, he continues.

"I've been investigating her murder since you told me about it," he starts.

"I knew that. You told me you were going to ask around, use your skills from debt collecting to see if you could dig anything up," I say, confused about how this is supposed to be a confession when I already knew he was looking into it.

"Right. So, I enlisted the help of a sort of private investigator. To your credit, you covered your tracks well, intentionally or not, because I was convinced, up until ten minutes ago, that Dawson had killed Emily as a sort of revenge plan for losing you," he says, a small smile playing at his lips.

Though everything still feels incredibly heavy, I return the smile, feeling slightly better than I have in weeks.

"However, this is where the confession part comes in," he states, wringing his hands together nervously now. I've rarely seen him nervous. When his eyes flit to mine, there's a hint of worry in them. In a blink, it's gone.

"I haven't been entirely honest with you either," he leads, holding my gaze. I feel my heart skip a beat before pounding in my chest as the anxiety rises to match my quick breaths.

"Okay..." I stretch out, impatiently waiting to be clued in to whatever it is he felt the need to confess.

"When I said I was a debt collector," he explains, "I was telling the truth. I just didn't elaborate. Several years back, I got involved with a man named James. In a world not so different than the one Emily was desperate to escape." I watch as he swallows, Adam's apple bobbing quickly. The nervousness is back. I can feel the hesitation from him across the room, which does nothing to ease my discomfort.

"James deals a lot in filthy things. Drugs. Sex work. Occasionally some gambling on a small scale. I don't agree with everything he does but I got myself out of a shitty life with his help, so I owe it to him when he needs work done and can't trust anyone else." He pauses to gauge my reaction, though I do my best to keep my composure and not give anything away. Easier said than done. "I take care of the problem for him when he needs loose ends tied up. I collect on some of these debts with lives."

The silence hangs between us for long seconds, weighted with the truth of our situations, both together and individually.

He sighs deeply. "You didn't scream and tell me to leave, or run away yourself, so I guess that's a good sign. As good as it's gonna get anyway." He stands and stretches his arms above his head, his shirt riding up to expose a few inches of his toned stomach and that delicious V that glides down from his hips.

He clears his throat, bringing me back to an absolutely embarrassing reality. I just confessed to murdering my best friend, followed by this gorgeous specimen of a man telling me about his dirty work, and all I can concentrate on is his physique. My cheeks redden at the thought and I can feel the color rising up my neck.

"Sorry," I apologize weakly. "You were saying?"

This gets a deep chuckle, making me even more embarrassed. I really want to crawl in a hole and die right now.

"I was just professing my undying love for the princess locked away in the tower, and how I managed to slay the three-headed dragon, which had never been done before might I add, in an attempt to impress her enough to run away with me and make me the happiest man on earth," he says, waving his arms around dramatically, slaying the pretend dragon all over again. "And here you were, daydreaming about a happily taken man." He rolls his eyes, eliciting a ridiculous belly laugh from me. The kind I haven't been capable of in I don't even know how long. Years probably.

"Oh, my sincerest apologies, your highness," I laugh, sweeping down toward the floor in a mock bow from where I sit in the chair. "It certainly won't happen again." I sit back up, pulling my knees to my chest. The sleeves of my sweatshirt cover my hands as I use them to cover the grin still plastered across my face.

I'm greeted with an overexaggerated eye roll, which keeps the smile glued to my face. "I was saying that I have more to confess, on a serious note," he says, all traces of the carefree laughter gone now. The air grows heavy again, thick with tension from his side.

"I told you about my actual debt collections, what that really entailed. But what I left out was my most recent assignment." He stops to take me in for a moment. This pause only adds to the gravity of the situation. I have a sick feeling taking root all of a sudden.

"James called me a while back with an important mission. I had taken some time off from collecting, trying to focus more on a respectable career and something I would enjoy. Something I could build a life around. That's how I ended up in editing and getting your original email about your manuscript, which was absolutely breathtaking by the way." A small proud smile spreads across his face, warming my soul. I didn't realize he had even taken the time to read it, especially after everything that's happened between us. Or not happened, rather.

"Anyway. This assignment. James asked me to take care of something personal for him. He was friends with Emily's father years ago. He got wind of the trouble she was in, with a rival no less. He was worried about her," he pauses, a look of shock spreading across my face. I had no idea her dad would have been involved with a man like this. He didn't seem the type.

"He asked me to bring Emily to him. So he could help her. Maybe get her out of this trouble and get her life back for her, as a repayment to her father. So, I started digging. I've found out over the years that getting close with a friend can be a gateway to the actual target," he states, head hung low with eyes on the floor.

The realization sinks in a few seconds later, feeling like it crushed my soul. We went from happy and laughing, to the realization that I was just a way to get to Emily. An easy passage.

"Wait, wait, wait," he says, throwing his hands up in protest. "Let me explain. It's not how that sounded." I sit in silence, mind whirling. It sounds cliché as fuck, even to myself, but I *really* thought we had something here.

"Honestly, Roman, I don't think there's anything else for us to talk about here." I push up out of my chair, tears stinging the backs of my eyes.

I make it to the kitchen before he catches me, pinning me to the counter with one arm on each side of my body, inches from me but making sure not to actually touch me. I refuse to look him in the eye. I know I'm acting childish, but the sting is real. Regardless of what has or hasn't happened between us, my growing feelings for him are real.

"You're wrong, Jade. We have everything to talk about. There's still so much to lay out," he persists, keeping me caged in. The tension is building again, making me miserably uncomfortable. I can't move without touching him. I'm not claustrophobic by any means, but I suddenly feel as if I can't breathe, sending me into a mini panic.

"Let me go, Roman," I plead quietly. I catch his eye, seeing a brief moment of sadness before something else entirely takes over. The look is damn near predatory. The way he's looking at me sets of an explosion of butterflies in my stomach, fluttering through my veins. *Holy fuck.*

I put my hand on his chest and push gently, trying to create some space. Instead of moving, though, his hand captures the one still holding onto the countertop, keeping me in place.

"Please talk to me," he asks softly, voice gentle regardless of what is in his eyes. "Please."

"Fine," I concede, pushing a little harder now. He steps back, releasing my hand. With a sigh of relief, I step farther away from him. Grabbing a couple glasses, I fill them with a delicious red wine, sure we will need the help to get through the rest of this talk. Handing one to him, I head back to my chair, hoping to stay in one piece until this is over.

His hand circles my wrist, pulling me onto the couch beside him. I don't fight, even though I need the space I was trying to create.

"I know how that sounded," he starts, eyes sincere and filled with anguish now. "I'm fully aware that it sounded like you were just an easy way to get to Emily. To accomplish this task I was given," he validates. "But I swear to you, Jade. On everything I've ever held as sacred, that's not what this is." The intensity of his voice has me faltering. There's no way he's faking that.

"I'll admit that at first, you were supposed to be an easy way in. I won't deny that. But from the moment I saw you in that gym, everything changed. And lord, when I actually got to speak to you and get to know you a little? Hell, it was over for me from the first time we spoke," he admits, looking shaken and unsure. "There was no going back for me. Not even for a second. Yes, I still had a job to do. That was still important. But that had nothing to do with you from that point on."

Noticing my shaking hands, I take a sip from my glass before placing it on the small table. I curl into myself, anticipation creeping in. I'm not sure how to feel anymore. One minute, he's telling me he used me to get to Emily. The next, he's telling me we had some sort of connection right off the bat.

"When you talked to me about her that night in the apartment, all I could feel was despair for everything you were going through. I wanted to fix it all. Take the pain away. Make it so nothing ever hurt you again," he rushes, words flying out one after another as if he can't speak them fast enough. "Although I would've never guessed you were actually the one to kill her," a sly smile plays at his lips, "I wanted nothing more than to fix it and every other problem that came your way."

Closing my eyes, I revel in the words pouring from him, trying to soak in the moment.

"The more time we've spent together, the more I've come to adore you." The admission comes easily, seeping into the marrow of my bones. I can physically feel the weight of them as they settle in.

"So what now?"

Chapter Eighteen

Roman

"So what now?" Jade asked, leaving the question hanging in the thick air between us, eyes locked on mine.

I take in the sight of her, doing my best to memorize every tiny detail. From the curve of her eyelashes, to the natural wave of her hair, all accentuating her gorgeous face. She's truly unlike any woman I've ever seen before.

The thought of this conversation being the last time I ever speak to her is enough to send me into a panic. She hasn't run for the hills or flew into a rage and kicked me out, so that's a good sign, but I'm not sure things have truly sunk in just yet either.

"Truly, I don't know," I answer, giving her the truth. I haven't ever been this vulnerable and honest with anybody. This is all uncharted territory for me, and I'm not sure how to navigate through it, especially given the gravity of the circumstances.

"Well," she says, a bit of pep back in her tone all of a sudden. "How about another glass of wine then? I feel like we probably have more to discuss and I don't know about you, but I've done all the talking I can do without a little liquid motivation." She plucks my glass from my hand, quietly walking to the kitchen.

The room feels different now. There's still a slight tension but it feels lighter, like things might just be okay in the end. A small smile appears on my face at the thought, erasing some of the worry from moments ago, even if we do still have things to figure out.

Like how to make sure she never gets caught. The thought creeps into my head, drowning out the bliss for a moment before I'm able to stuff it back down into the depths of my subconscious. I've had enough worry for one day. I'll spend my time worrying about that when I can actually do something about it. For now, I fully plan to immerse myself in her presence, forgetting everything else for the time being.

"How about something a little less depressing for the rest of the night?" she asks, rejoining me on the couch. She's much more relaxed now, sipping her wine as she settles into the soft cushions.

"What did you have in mind?" I ask, eyebrow raised as my mind speeds through the possibilities. I can feel the heat coursing through my blood and I'm not sure if it's from the alcohol or being so close to her. Either way, it's definitely from an intoxication of one form or another.

"Let's play truth or dare," she suggests, a bright smile lighting her face for the first time all evening. This one actually reaches her eyes, furthering my intoxication to the point that a goofy smile stretches across my face. She's nearly vibrating with excitement beside me, the energy contagious.

"Okay," I laugh, giving in to whatever keeps her smiling and happy like this. Somewhere deep inside, I realize I will always do whatever it takes to keep her this happy. The thought is terrifying. "You go first."

"Truth or dare?" she asks with a wiggle of her eyebrow, making me laugh out loud. I've never seen someone so cute.

"Hmm. Truth." Her disappointment is instant.

"Loser," she chides, rolling her eyes. "Umm.. what's your biggest fear?"

Not being with you. "Heights, of course," I respond, not at all the truth. "Truth or dare?"

"Dare." The happiness is back, masking the earlier disappointment at my choice.

"I dare you to... do the thing you're most afraid of right —" Without a second's hesitation, her lips are on mine. I don't even have time to blink before she's back in her seat, eyes filled with heat and temptation.

I don't have a clue what I was expecting, maybe something to do with heights or spiders, clowns even. It absolutely was not that, and I'm stunned silent.

Without skipping a beat, she continues, asking the same question to keep the game going.

"Truth. Again," I say, knowing the backlash I'll get but unable to pick the risky choice.

Another eye roll. "How did you feel about that?" She pulls her bottom lip between her teeth, enchantment washing over me as I watch it. I glance at her eyes to find her watching me as I watch her.

"Surprised," I respond simply. It's the truth, but I don't elaborate, keeping the answer short. "Truth or dare."

"Truth."

"Well, how the mighty have fallen," I joke, thankful she has released that lip now. "Tell me about your dreams of the future." I watch as a wistful expression cloaks her features, like she's being pulled into a happier time far away.

"I try not to dream," she says, voice tinged with a sadness that pulls at my heart. "But when I do... I dream of a modest house in the mountains, where I can sit on the back porch and enjoy the view while I drink my wine. Off white, black shudders. Huge picture windows in the back. Homey, comfortable. With a library, of course, so I can work on my writing and read until my heart's fulfilled." The look on her face is one of pure contentment, yet still full of longing.

"All by yourself?" I ask, forgetting about the game as I find myself wrapped up in her dreams.

"Those aren't the rules, Roman," she scolds, though the smile on her face is anything but serious. "Only one question at a time. It's your turn to choose now."

"Dare." I say, taking the risk and silently praying I don't regret it.

"About damn time," she chuckles before taking another sip of wine. "I dare you to do something you've wanted to do for a long time but haven't had the confidence to do yet."

She's gonna be the death of me. I move slowly, wrapping my hand around her upper arm as I pull her over toward me. I pull my leg up and over her before pulling her against me so her back is laying flush against my chest with one of my legs on either side of her.

Her content sigh has my heart reeling into a free fall, destined for death when I hit the bottom. But I'll be damned if I'm not going to enjoy the fall.

"Truth or dare?" I coax in her ear, barely above a whisper. I see the tiny bumps rise on her neck, giving her away.

"Umm. I'm going to go with... dare."

"Such a risk taker," I joke. "I dare you to tell me how you're feeling right now."

"Fuck. Truth? Changed my mind."

"That's not how this works," I chuckle, readjusting underneath her so we fit together more snugly. She leans her head back against my shoulder, relaxing into me finally.

"Cheater," she says, and I swear I can hear the eye roll, even if she is being playful. "I'm feeling... scared. Overwhelmed. Confused. A lot," she admits, careful not to say too much.

"I completely get that. Want to talk about it? Maybe we can talk it out and get you feeling better," I suggest, hating that she's feeling that way. I was hoping for a different answer entirely.

"I'm not even sure where to start," she admits, taking another sip and frowning when she finds her glass nearly empty now. "This whole thing between us, whatever this is, has been so complicated. Sometimes I feel like we have something, then it turns around and it's like I never existed to you. It makes my head spin." I have a feeling the alcohol is making her a little braver than she would normally be. Truthfully, she's the bravest and boldest person I know when it comes to anything except feelings. Those don't seem to be her strong suit.

"You're totally right. It has been complicated," I agree, running my fingertips over the back of her hand lightly. "But that's been because I was pushing you away. Trying to find a way to not get close to you. The hardest I pushed you away, the more I wanted you though. I wasn't being honest with you because I was afraid the truth would push you away for good."

She sits up now, turning to face me on the couch. As scary as this conversation is, it needs to happen, and it feels good to finally get it off my chest.

"The honest to god's truth is I'm not a good man, Jade. I've done some truly horrible, disgusting things. Things nobody should be capable of doing, and it's made me feel like a monster for years. I don't want you to be affected in any way by that," I say, holding her gaze.

"That's bullshit, Roman. You don't get to decide for me, especially by keeping me in the fucking dark!" She's pissed, and I can't say I even blame her. She takes a huge inhale, holds it in, then slowly exhales through her nose until I'm positive there can't be even a molecule of oxygen left in her lungs.

"Never mind. It doesn't even matter now. I wasn't completely honest with you either. Neither of us were anywhere close to perfect in this whole freaking mess." She seems frustrated now as she pulls her knees to her chest and rests her cheek on them, no longer looking at me.

"So what now?" I echo her question from earlier. I can feel myself starting to spiral inside, mostly from fear of the unknown and where this might be headed. I've never needed a single soul in this life, not since I was 15 and had to figure shit out for myself. But I *need* her.

The realization hits like a ton of bricks, and I'm suddenly queasy, the alcohol not sitting well at all. This is bad.

"What do you want?" she asks simply, raising her head to look at me once more.

"You," I answer instantly.

"And what if I'm too much? Or not enough?" she questions, eyes starting to fill with unshed years of insecurities. "What if I get caught?" The question is no more than a whisper, the gravity of our situation settling in.

"You won't," I answer honestly. I'm sure the police will eventually piece it all together, if they care to dig that deep, but I'll make damn sure there are never any repercussions for her actions. "I want you, all of you, no matter the cost. No matter the situation. No matter how happy, how heart-wrenchingly devastating. I want you, or nothing at all."

She sniffles before throwing herself at me, pushing me back against the armrest of the couch as her body molds to mine once again. I'm overtaken by a feeling of home. Complete. Final.

Fuck. So this is what it feels like to find your person.

Snuggling her head into my shoulder to hide her teary eyes, she wraps her arms around my body, holding on like she's found a life raft in the middle of the ocean. Her only hope for making it home safe. It's not long before sniffles are accompanying the sounds of our breathing, and it shatters my heart.

"Hey, look at me," I coax, pushing gently against her shoulders in a weak attempt to persuade her. Shaking her head emphatically, she lays down against me again, finding a little comfort in our closeness. Instead of pushing the issue, I rub my palms down her back slowly, begging the gods to bring her some semblance of peace.

"Why would you want me?" she asks meekly. "After all the things I admitted to doing. I killed my best friend, for the love of all things holy. There's no redemption for somebody like me. No happy endings here." The ache in her voice is soul crushing. Even worse than the ache is the fact that she fully believes that line of bullshit.

"Do you think I'm capable of being saved? Worthy of being loved and happy and fulfilled?" I ask, genuinely curious. If she feels that way about the one death she's responsible for, I can only imagine how she feels about the things I've done.

She shoots straight up like a rocket, sparks of rage dancing across her tear-streaked face. "Of course I do! You're absolutely worthy of all of those things and so much more. Regardless of how you feel about yourself, you are a good man, Roman. You did what you had to do to survive, and I'd even gamble to say you're better for the wicked and terrible things you've done. You're stronger because of the things you've had to do. Doing what you had to do doesn't make you any less worth of redemption or love than anyone else."

She's panting by the time she steps down off the soapbox, anger dissipating slowly as the reality of what she just said takes hold.

"Holy fuck," is her only response.

"Exactly. You did what you *had to do* in order to survive, Jade. Literally. Had Emily gotten as far as trading you to those men, I can guarantee without a sliver of doubt in my wretched soul that you would not have survived. I know some of those men personally. Those men truly are monsters. They find a sick pleasure in doing unspeakable things, especially to women, before they slice their throats, dismember their bodies, and get rid of any evidence they ever existed in this world." The disgust that crosses her face is justified, as well as the fear. She has no clue how close she came to a gruesome death.

We sit in a weighted silence, neither of us sure what to say now. Things could've ended up very differently. But here we are, together, talking openly for the first time. Maybe there is some hope after all.

She lays her head on the throw pillow, her feet now pulled up on the middle section of the couch next to mine. "Truth or dare?" she asks, eliciting a ludicrous laugh from me.

"Truth?" I say, half statement, half question.

"Do you really think we're going to be okay in the end?" she asks, barely able to voice the question.

I pause, not at all wanting to break the honesty we've had going for us tonight, but I don't dare to tell her the entire truth now. She's been through too much tonight. "I think we will figure it out, no matter what comes our way. Come hell or high water."

She nods lightly, snuggling down further into the couch. The exhaustion from everything that transpired tonight pulls her under within minutes. When her soft breaths take on steady rhythm, I find a fuzzy blanket and cover her, tucking it in around her.

With a gentle kiss to her forehead, careful not to rouse her, I settle in with a blanket of my own, feeling anxious but ready to take on whatever is coming for us in the days ahead.

This girl deserves the world, and I'm hellbent on giving it to her with no regard for the cost.

Chapter Nineteen

Jade

I wake with a jolt, heart pounding in my ears, skin covered in a cold sweat. In the dimly lit living room, I'm able to make out a form on the other end of the couch, breathing steadily.

It takes a full ten seconds to register that it's Roman on the couch opposite of me. When that fact sets in, I put my hand to my chest, covering my pounding heart.

I'm so damn jumpy lately, I chastise in my head, shaking it slowly to clear the terror that has resigned there for way too long now.

My breathing slows over the course of the next couple minutes, lulling me into a peaceful state as I watch the beginnings of the sunrise from where I lie. That damn nightmare pulled me out of deep sleep yet again, same as most every night lately. But I feel more energized and better than I have in weeks this morning.

It's oddly comforting to know he stayed last night, even after everything was laid out on the table. By the end, we were both baring scars, old and new, for the other to examine. Bleeding freely, openly expectant of the other to walk away instead of bathing in the blood of our shared atrocities.

At the end of the night, our fates seemed sealed and intimately intertwined. Only time will tell, of course, but there was something special about last night. Like a final puzzle piece clicking into place.

My eyes bounce between the sunrise and Roman, sleeping peacefully still. As much as I don't want to disturb him, I'm itching to be close to him again, so I shift over to his side of the couch, climbing underneath the cover and flush with his warm body.

Without hesitation, he wraps his arm around me, pulling me closer than I could have imagined possible.

"Good morning, beautiful," he says, voice thick with sleep. The low hum of his voice sets my blood on fire.

"I'm sorry," I apologize. "I wasn't trying to wake you. I just wanted to be close." I turn my head to try to catch a glimpse of his gorgeous features. He's absolutely mesmerizing when he's totally content.

"Don't ever apologize for that," he says, nuzzling his nose into my neck.

"Go back to sleep," I say, instead of spewing the apology that's still dancing on the tip of my tongue.

"Not a snowball's chance in hell," he says, running his hand lightly up and down my arm. "You look flawless in the sunrise. I wouldn't want to miss this view for the world."

I can't even fight the smile that takes over my face, threatening to split my head in half. Instead, I roll my eyes, feeling half drunk from the exchange.

He's still nuzzling against my neck when he plants one chaste kiss there. It nearly does me in. I swear, if I had been standing, my knees would have betrayed me with that one simple gesture.

This man has some sort of voodoo power over me that I've never experienced before. I'm definitely no virgin, but I have never been so easily affected by any man in my life.

I roll halfway over to face him, effectively cutting off his access to my neck. Hopefully not giving too much away at the same time.

"Let me make you breakfast?" I ask, hand cupping his strong jaw which now has a fine stubble coating it. Looking into those gorgeous eyes, I can't help but get a little lost. He looks so happy, like nothing is wrong in the world.

Like we haven't both murdered people.

I banish the thought before it has a chance to ruin the moment. Thoughts of what I've done have ruined basically every waking and non-waking moment for me recently, and I refuse to let them have this one too. For right now, I'm being entirely selfish.

Zoning back into reality, I push up off the couch and head to the kitchen. "Alexa," I say, "play Rain by Sleep Token." I sway gently, letting the music consume me, as I start pulling things from the fridge. Eggs, bacon, sausage, canned biscuits.

I start some gravy from scratch, just like my nana taught me when I was a kid. Completely lost in the work and music, I jump as Roman comes up behind me, wrapping his arms around my stomach and pressing himself into my back. A slow smile forms as I lean my head back against his shoulder, more content than I've ever been.

For a bittersweet moment, I imagine a future with this man. The house, the career, the laughter and tears. The journey. That's the sweet part. Filtering in quickly after are the thoughts of how this is almost assuredly going to end. Going up in flames, burning us both beyond recognition.

Chokehold begins playing, continuing the Sleep Token mood, and it couldn't be more fitting. Between Rain and Chokehold, it describes our budding relationship perfectly. Intoxicating but doomed from the beginning if we were to be totally honest with ourselves.

Instead, I hang onto the thread of hope like it's the last breath of oxygen I'll ever pull into my lungs. This man awakens something inside me that has been asleep for far too long, nearly forgotten all together. A piece of me that feels hopeful, happy to still be here on this earth. Content to deal with the trials and hardships coming my way just to get the chance to be held by him one more time. The thought has the back of my throat burning, tears threatening to fill my eyes.

Clearing my throat, I wiggle my way out of his hold, determined to put some space between us before it's too late to do so. As much as I'd love to stay in his arms forever, I can't afford to get too attached, especially with everything we have to face.

"Do you mind to watch this for just a minute? I need to go to the bathroom," I explain, walking away from the stove and my future, feeling the shutdown coming on.

There's a heavy concern in his eyes as he nods, watching me go. I feel his eyes on me as I make my way through the living room to the bedroom, willing myself to keep putting one foot in front of the other.

Pushing the bathroom door gently until I hear the quiet click, I breathe a sigh of relief as my eyes fill with tears, the strangest mix of happiness, terror, and grief. I feel as if my heart is simultaneously being ripped from my chest and beating with a new purpose. The feeling is overwhelming, threatening to take me under in a swift panic.

Easing myself to the floor, leaning back against the door, I pull my knees up, cradling them to my chest, hoping to soothe the sensation building up inside it. It's harder to pull in full breaths now. My throat feels tight, heart flip flopping inside my ribcage. The feeling is so violent and tumultuous I wonder if I'm on the verge of a heart attack.

All the breathing exercises in the world couldn't save me from the panic building in my blood. I try breathing in through my nose, out slowly through my mouth. Inhale for eight, hold for four, exhale for four. Internally, the only change is a rapid rise in panic and my heart rate.

So instead of fighting it, I give in, letting it take over me. My mind races, consuming me entirely. Thoughts of Emily, of Dawson, both the past and the future, Roman, all of it races through my mind. The feeling is overwhelming, like climbing to the top of a skyscraper and jumping. A total freefall destined for death at the end.

A small knock sounds behind me. I'm far too lost in my head to even acknowledge it. "You okay?" he says soothingly, voice soft and quiet. I shake my head silently, unable to use my voice, knowing it would break and give me away. I angrily wipe at a tear as it makes its way down my cheek to join the others that have collected on my shirt.

"Can I come in?" He doesn't turn the knob or try to open the door. Simply asks for my acceptance, then waits, letting me keep some semblance of control in the spiral. I breathe out loudly, a rush of air leaving my body, along with what's left of my resolve.

I stand on shaky legs, swiping at my reddened cheeks and puffy eyes. I look absolutely ridiculous, but the visual is a good representation for how I'm feeling at the moment.

Broken, ugly, and scarred. Not good enough. Incapable and undeserving.

Wrapping my hand around the round knob, I lean my forehead against the door, entirely unsure if I'm ready to face him but knowing I can't hide in here forever. I twist the knob and pull the door toward me slowly. When the door opens, my jaw hits the floor, heart leaping inside my chest.

Holy fuck. I was not expecting this.

Chapter Twenty

Roman

"Can I come in?" I had asked, waiting patiently for her answer. I didn't want to push her too hard or make the situation any worse than it already was. Something had flipped in her all of a sudden, shifting from happy and content to something else I couldn't quite put my finger on. She was fine one second, and fighting tears the next. When she excused herself, I had felt a surge of panic, followed by a crushing helplessness.

As she opened the bathroom door, I could see her red cheeks and swollen eyes. Tear streaks were still painted across her face, eyes still watery. She looked absolutely stunning, despite being upset. Hell, I think half of her beauty in that moment was *because* of that upset. She was raw, completely authentic. Vulnerable.

As her jaw falls open in surprise, I take a small step back, allowing her to survey the room. During her time in the bathroom, I made quick work of breakfast before setting it up for her in the bedroom. There is food, juice, and coffee, all prepared for her when she's ready.

The tears return to her eyes, along with a look of astonishment. My heart beats a little faster, happy I could do this for her. She nearly tackles me as she throws her arms around my neck, forcing me to take a couple stumbling steps backward.

"Thank you," she whispers into my neck with a small sniffle. "Thank you for everything."

I tighten my grip around her, adoring the feeling of her body close to mine. "It's nothing," I say sheepishly, not being used to having someone's appreciation. In my line of work, most things go unnoticed unless you fuck something up. As long as you're doing everything you're supposed to, you remain a ghost.

She pulls back, a look of frustration crossing her face. Her eyebrows are pinched together as she considers what to say. "That's bullshit," she starts, diving right in. "This is the sweetest thing anyone has ever done for me."

"Well, you're welcome. You deserve it. I wasn't really sure how to help, and this was the first thing that popped in my head, so here we are," I say, feeling like I need to explain. "I didn't feel like you would want to talk much, so I thought maybe this would help ease your mind when you were ready to face the world again."

I can see the stress leave her body as she sighs, even though her eyes are still lost and watery. She looks tired but a little less panicked now. As she looks back into my eyes, I can see the relief filter in. I just pray that relief isn't as short-lived as I fear it may be.

"Seriously. Thank you," she repeats, hugging me again. "It means the world to me that you took the time to do this for me, just to give me something to smile about after the rain stopped."

"I would burn down the entire world just to put a smile on your face, Jade. Without a single shred of remorse."

She takes the words in stride, not really absorbing the depth of their truth. The words fall on her ears as an empty promise, meaning no more than the breath they were spoken on.

"Eat," I say, taking her soft hand and leading her to the bed. Once she gets comfortable, I place the tray in front of her and watch as she picks at the food. "Eat," I say again, more stern this time. "We have some things to do today, and you're going to need your energy." I wave away her questions as she begins to eat more enthusiastically.

However, if she knew what I have in mind, I don't think she would be in such a hurry. Just because I said we have things to do doesn't mean they're going to be enjoyable in the slightest. But necessary all the same.

I can't have her being caught for Emily's murder so we need to cover her tracks quickly. The police aren't doing much in the way of investigating right now, but should a tip come in or a detective get a wild hair, it wouldn't be all that hard to find out the truth. Hell, I did it fairly quickly with just a few resources.

She pulls me back to reality, asking what we need to do once again. "I'll explain on the way, but you have to finish your breakfast first."

***

It's an unusually crisp fall morning as we make our way toward James's office. It takes about an hour to drive there, assuming there's not a lot of traffic. Lucky for us, there weren't many people on the road today. As we exit the Audi, I zip my jacket up to my chin to beat off the chilly breeze as Jade wraps her arms around her chest.

Watching her hair blow in the breeze as the red and yellow leaves fall behind her makes me wish we were anywhere but here. A quiet walk through the park, a picnic once the sun comes out to warm the air a bit. Anywhere else.

But this is a necessary evil. I just wish the churning in my stomach would relax before I hurl up the breakfast I scarfed down before leaving her apartment. I'm not entirely sure how this meeting will go, considering she's the one who murdered his best friend's daughter, but I don't have anyone else to turn to. No one I trust at least. If we're going to get out of this mess, I need James on my side.

Trusting my gut, I tap on the metal door, watching a few flecks of rust make their way to the ground. The building looks entirely abandoned if you don't know better. It's not in a great part of town, so it's a good cover. Most businesses here went under several years ago when the economy went belly up.

The door slowly creaks open, hinges whining loudly. Otto stands behind the door, sinister as ever. His 6'5" form towers above me, even though I'm not short at 6'3" but his entire aura makes him feel like an impenetrable monster. Simply breathing the same air as him is nothing short of terrifying.

I stand frozen, doing my best to keep my breathing completely even. I swear he's like a dog and can smell fear from a mile away.

"Who's she?" Otto asks, deep voice reverberating in the empty space of the warehouse. He doesn't much more than glance at Jade before his full attention is turned back to me.

"A friend," I answer simply. I can feel her glare burning a hole into the back of my head, but it's best to not give any information that could ever be used against us, especially when I'm not sure how this is going to pan out. Coming here might have been a colossal mistake.

"Right. Mighty fine friend you've got there," Otto says, hoping to pull a reaction from me to give us away. When I step back and extend my hand in a 'go ahead' gesture, she nearly unravels with fury, though she keeps her face mostly calm and collected.

Instead, he steps aside, ushering us further into the dusty building, away from the safety outside these walls. I swallow past the lump forming in my throat, making my way through the empty room to the stairs in the back. The metal creaks beneath our feet as we slowly ascend to the platform of the upper level, overlooking the rest of the warehouse.

With a deep breath, I turn to the wooden door on my right and raise my hand to knock. Three knocks, then wait. Just like every other time I've visited. James has a very specific way of doing things and I've found it's best to follow that to the letter, especially if you're needing to ask a favor.

"Come in," his gruff voice sounds from behind the door. Turning the knob, I'm nearly knocked over with a wave of anxiousness as I step into the dimly lit office.

James is sitting behind his desk, laptop open in front of him, no doubt tracking some poor soul's whereabouts. There's a small lamp with a stained-glass lampshade on the far corner of the desk that Emily picked out for him when she was a child. He told me that story as he relayed my most recent task the last time I was here. The memory makes my mouth go dry.

He looks up at me from behind the screen, a small familiar smile gracing his features. Hell, it even reaches his eyes for once. Until he sees I'm not alone at least. The smile instantly fades, replaced with a scowl and contempt. He's not a fan of new people, to say the least.

He raises one eyebrow, turning his attention back to me, waiting for answers to questions unasked. "She's a friend," I explain. This time, there's no glare burning into the back of my head. Jade is standing stock-still, terrified of the man before us. And for good reason. "I don't want to waste any of your time. But we've come here to ask a favor."

This piques his interest, the hostility leaving his eyes. James loves favors. Everything comes with a price. The more desperate you are for the favor, the higher the price. Except this time, he actually owes me so I'm calling in a favor, not the other way around.

Once upon a time, years ago, James himself wasn't in such a prime position. He was at the end of his rope, nothing left to his name. The small group of men he had built up around him to do his dirty work had left him high and dry when the money ran out. His wife had left him for the man she was having an affair with, citing James never being available as the reason for her infidelity.

Everything he had worked so hard for – literal blood, sweat, and tears – came crashing down around him. The poor man couldn't even afford to feed himself for a little while.

During that time, I had decided to stick around. Honestly, I felt sorry for the guy. I had no idea he would rebound and become entirely ruthless in the process. Prior to the downfall, he actually had a little bit of empathy for people and put a ladder down into the holes they had dug for themselves to try to help them get back on their feet.

He stayed with me for a couple months, until he was able to collect on a few debts and get some money rolling again. Once that happened, he bought this place for pennies on the dollar after the businesses around it went under. Since then, he's been absolutely heartless, leaving a bloody trail everywhere he goes.

The memory is still fresh in my mind when he speaks again. "So what's this favor you're after?" he asks, a sly smile slithering across his face. "And what's it worth to you?" He steeples his fingers on the desk in front of him, looking every bit the predator I know him to be.

"I'm calling in a favor, James. I'm not looking to make one of your deals today," I say, doing my best to keep the shake out of my voice. I both fear and respect this man, and I've been heavily dreading the day I needed to cash in on this.

"Oh? And how would you think to get out of a deal?" His eyebrow raises, confusion lacing his eyes.

"You know as well as I do. You remember the conversation we had about you owing me one all those years ago, James. I'd rather not bring up the details with company."

He's challenging me, wanting to see if I'll stick to my guns instead of falling to my knees before him like most of his men do. But this time, I will. There's too much at stake, and I can't repay whatever price he would put on this one.

"That's fair," he agrees after a few tense seconds. I can feel the sweat that had beaded along my neck start to cool now, a little less anxious than I was five seconds ago. "What do you need?" He leans back in his chair, the metal making an awful screeching sound that has me wanting to cover my ears.

"I need you to be open-minded with this one," I start, nervous about how he's going to take all of this.

He nods, eyes cautious, but he doesn't stop me.

"Here goes," I say on an exhale. "This is my friend, Jade," I continue, looking over to her. She looks more terrified than I've ever seen her, but she stands as tall as she can, not wanting to give that away. She knows fear is a weakness in this world, so she's putting her bravest face on, despite how she feels.

"She managed to get herself into a really fucked up situation a little while back. But here's where I need you to be open-minded and hear me out," I explain, pausing until his eyes return to mine.

"She killed her best friend. Normally I don't agree with the whole 'it was self-defense' bullshit excuse, but I've looked over every shred of evidence and gone through all the details personally. This one truly was self-defense. She didn't have any other option." I pause for another second before adding the sentence that could send this whole plan into a heaping disaster.

"Her best friend was Emily St. John." I can damn near see the other shoe drop as his face contorts with a rage I haven't often seen from him. The sound that rips from his lungs is otherworldly, a roar of anger and pain so intense I feel it as it makes its way through my body.

Not only have I completely failed my mission, therefore failing him, but I also brought the woman who killed his best friend's daughter into his warehouse to ask for a favor. To protect her nonetheless.

I should've known better.

"What the FUCK do you mean *she* killed Emily?! And that it was self-defense?! Have you lost your fucking mind, Roman?" he screams, the sound echoing off the walls.

For several tense seconds, I let him rage. I let him feel whatever emotions are coursing through his body right now as he takes the information in.

Once he starts to slow, the anger seeping from his pores instead of radiating from them now, I try again.

"James, you're a logical man. I know that. I brought some of the information with me on this thumb drive," I say, pulling the device from the front pocket of my jeans. "I knew you wouldn't take my word for it, but let me show you."

I reach out toward the desk cautiously, placing the thumb drive on the edge, not daring to put my limbs any closer to this man than is absolutely necessary. I watched him chop a man's hand off in less than a second once before, and while I don't see any weapons capable of that within reach, I don't want to take the chance. I wouldn't look good with a pirate hook for a hand.

He takes the thumb drive, eyeing me with a mix of curiosity and doubt, along with maybe a dash of hatred. Plugging it in, he clicks the file that pops up.

"You'll find the texts between Emily and Jade's ex-boyfriend, Dawson. The texts allude to some other plan, aside from the cheating. You'll also find the coroner's report, police report, and cell phone location reports for both Emily and Jade's phones during that day." I give him a few minutes to look through everything before mentioning the final piece of evidence I was able to pull together last night when I wasn't able to sleep.

"Lastly, you'll find Emily's text messages. Pick any number of them, they're all basically the same. In those, you'll find that she was making arrangements with Cain to sell Jade as a repayment for her debts." The shock on his face is undeniable, only growing in intensity as he reads those incriminating messages.

"Damn," he says finally, closing the laptop. "I've seen enough. I don't want to think of her that way, not when I watched that kid grow up." He stops for a moment, seemingly lost in the memories of her childhood. "I was supposed to protect her," he says, pulling his head up in resignation. "But

I can see she was way farther gone than I could've ever seen coming."

"I'm so sorry," I say sincerely, hating that everyone in this room has been harmed in some way by her selfish actions. Jade has tears in her eyes now, but she holds her head high, refusing to allow them to fall for her former life.

"I came here to ask you for protection for Jade. I know Emily is gone, meaning there's no real reason for Cain to try to come for Jade now, but I don't trust it. He's fucked up. I was hoping for protection, and maybe a little helping throwing the police off her trail, should they get close to figuring it all out," I rush out, not sure I'd be able to continue if I stopped at any point.

He takes his time considering my proposition, rising from his chair and leisurely strolling around the room. Even that simple act feels threatening. I can feel the fury still coming from him, though it's been diluted now. The betrayal cuts deep.

"Stand," he orders, both of us immediately rising from our chairs. He pulls me into a long hug, almost fatherly, before quickly hugging Jade as well. "I'm very sorry for what happened to you. For all you've gone through. Truly, I am. However, I can't offer you my protection," he says, looking torn but sticking to his guns. "Emily was like a daughter to me. I'm shocked at the things she did, but I can't offer protection or help to the one responsible for her death."

My jaw goes slack, shocked that he's denying her even after all the evidence I provided, showing him exactly who Emily was at the end. *Fuck.*

"I can't help you, but I won't harm you either," he continues, offering a salve for the sting of rejection. "I won't hunt you down or hurt you in any way. I won't help the police find you. There's not much I could do to cover your tracks, but I won't aid in you being found out." He hugs her again, longer this time.

"As for you, Roman," he begins, turning back toward me. "It truly pains me to say our time together has run its course." He must see the pain flash through my eyes, my chest feeling like it's going to implode at any second. I feel like I've been gutted.

"Wait. What? Why? You've lost your mind, James," I begin, hating how close I sound to begging. This has been such a big part of my life, and I don't have a clue how to go forward without this part of it.

"I can't work with you from here on out, son. You'll be a liability. It's obvious that she means a great deal to you, especially if you were willing to bring her here and ask for my help, knowing how I've felt about Emily and her father. Knowing the assignment you were on. I'm sorry, but our time together is done." He hugs me one last time as a single tear slips from my eye, down onto the shoulder of his button up shirt.

Wiping my eye clear of any emotional evidence, I stand up straight, doing my best to respect his decision. I chose her, therefore choosing to end my career and relationship with James. I made this bed, so it's time to lie in it.

"If you'll so kindly see your way out. You know the way," he says, slipping back into his desk chair before handing me the thumb drive and gesturing to the door.

Chapter Twenty-One

Jade

Once we're outside of James's office, another man, skinnier and shorter than the first guy we dealt with, leads us back to the front door. Although, that wasn't necessary, as I could see it from the landing outside the office. Precautions, I guess.

The guy smelled of stale cigarettes and body odor, like he hadn't showered in close to a week, which might be true judging by his greasy hair. It takes actual effort to keep myself from gagging as we're being led to the door.

"Been nice working with you, man," the guy says, reaching his hand out to shake Roman's.

Roman doesn't hesitate to extend his hand, taking the guard's hand in a firm but friendly shake. "You too, Finn. Don't hesitate to call if you ever need something. You know I've got your back," he says before placing his hand on my lower back and ushering me back out onto the abandoned street.

The walk back to the car is radio silence. Not a sound from either of us, nor a sound from anywhere around us. No dogs, birds, people. Literally silent. It feels... wrong.

I do my best to shake the feeling as Roman opens the car door and I slide into the passenger seat. Back to mock safety.

After that little meeting, I don't feel any better. If anything, I honestly feel worse. Seeing this side of him has made his confession *very* real. I fully believed him at his word, but seeing him operate in this place allowed everything to click into place.

Most of the car ride back to his apartment is silent, minus him asking if I was hungry. Truly, I hadn't had the first thought about food. Now that he had asked, I felt ravenous, albeit a little nauseous from the day's events.

As we pull up to the apartment building, I'm nearly drooling from the smell of the food as we make our way to his door. We settled on a little diner with fresh burgers and fries, and the smell wafting from the dinner boxes is nothing short of magical.

The silence persists as we make our way up to his apartment. He unlocks the door, holding it open for me to go inside, before following me and locking the deadbolt behind us.

Once in the kitchen, I separate the food, handing him his box before grabbing two bottles of water from the fridge and settling in at the island. The exhaustion and silence both weigh in on me now that I've had time to start processing everything that's happened today. The feeling of the cool tabletop against my forearms slowly brings me back to reality, calming the anxiety raging through my veins.

We've done very little talking thus far since our stop at his former boss's place. There doesn't feel like there's a lot to say about it truthfully. It was pretty cut and dry from my perspective.

James isn't willing to help us. Fuck, I can't even blame him. I killed his best friend's daughter, and regardless of the reason, that's enough to turn damn near anybody away from helping you get out of the mess you made.

But it does make me feel a tad bit better to know that he isn't going to come after me for it. Even if that means Roman can never work with him again. Even if he loses the only group of people he's been close with since his childhood.

As the guilt sets in, I begin to pick at my food. From ravenous and starving to barely picking at it and feeling gross and uneasy in a moment's time.

Roman must notice because he slows his pace on his food as well, watching me carefully. I force a small smile, hoping to placate him long enough for him to finish his dinner. There's plenty of time for talking afterward.

"So that was a lot, huh?" he asks around a bite of his burger. His tongue snakes out to clear the bit of ketchup clinging to the side of his mouth. I smile a bit at that, caught off guard by how normal that action was while this conversation and our day has been anything but.

"Definitely a lot," I agree easily, closing the lid of the to-go box, appetite nowhere to be found now. "I had no idea Emily's dad was tied up in anything like this. He always seemed so... average," I say with a shrug. "I never would've guessed that in a million lifetimes. But I guess that's true of Emily too. I saw her damn near every day and had no clue, never even the slightest inclination, that something was going on with her. No clue she was in so much trouble."

My hands lie lifeless on the countertop as I stare down at them, thinking of all the times we painted our nails together. Held hands while we skipped through the hallways at school. These hands braided her hair on hundreds of occasions.

The grief that filters in is excruciating. It steals the air from my lungs, making it feel impossible to breathe. The pain is palpable, ripping through me in waves as it threatens to drown me.

"It's all my fault," I say in resolution. It wasn't intended as a cue for him to soothe me, or to tell me how I was wrong and that wasn't true. It was simply a statement. It truly is all my fault. That Emily is dead and he has now lost everyone he cares about.

"Listen. You did exactly what you had to do. Yes, you killed her. There's no denying that fact." He says it calmly but not coldly. Like he's talking about the weather outside. "But it was necessary." He levels his gaze with mine, driving the point home.

"You lost everyone. Because of me. Because of what I did," I say, keeping my gaze locked with his.

"I lost those people, yes. But I lost those people because I chose *you,* Jade. No one made me make that choice. I did it freely and without regret. And should it come to it, I'll make the exact same choice a million fucking times over." The sincerity in his voice has me breaking, walls crumbling down around me.

I had never known what it was like to truly be chosen by someone before.

I clear my throat, intent on keeping the depth of the emotions his words pulled from me to myself for the time being. "So how do we go forward from here?" I ask, hellbent on changing the subject. I'm not one to dwell on my feelings for long, especially when other people are around.

"I have a plan," he starts. "But it's risky as hell."

Chapter Twenty-Two

Roman

"Let's hear it," she says without hesitation. We've moved from the kitchen to the living room now, having cleared away the rest of our dinner.

Jade is curled up on one side of the couch, feet pulled up underneath her, eagerly awaiting my explanation. I opted for the opposite side, facing her so we can talk things through.

This is a really bad idea, my gut seems to be screaming. *There's no way this is going to pan out well for us.*

I exhale the deep breath I had been holding, reluctant to tell her my plan but unable to come up with anything else that has even the slightest chance of getting us out of this mess.

"It's sketchy at best, and to be entirely honest, it could put us in a worse position in the end," I begin. "I need to check with Sara to see if she can find out where the police stand on everything right now. Whether they're still looking or if they're any closer to figuring out that you killed her. That's the first step."

She nods but stays silent, eyes remaining dry. That's progress. She hasn't been able to hear of Emily's death and her part in it without breaking down until now.

"From there, we will have to make a choice. If they are closer to finding you, we only have one real option as far as I can see." Scrubbing my hand down my face and across the stubble on my jaw, I resign myself to the facts of the situation. "I need to get in contact with a couple of the guys I worked with. James's guys. I could probably count on them to help us out, help cover our tracks and get the police away from the evidence trail. Plant new evidence somehow."

"They would do that for you? Even after everything today?" she asks, doubt covering her face. "And how would they plant new evidence? This case started weeks ago. Without having an inside guy, I don't see how they would manage that." She shifts uncomfortably.

"Those are the easy parts truly. People will do most anything for the right price. The hard part is keeping it from getting back to James. He's ruthless when it comes to anything he feels is a betrayal. And his guys helping us after he kicked us out today? That would be the ultimate betrayal, both from us and from them. The punishment would be... brutal, to say the least." I can see the hesitation in her eyes, shadowed across her face. Who could blame her? This is a death sentence if it goes wrong, which is likely.

The only other option is to wait it out and hope for the best. Hope the police let it go cold, which I don't feel is likely. In a town this size, murder never happens. They're going to be desperate to get this one solved, whether it's now or five years from now. At some point, it's going to lead them to her doorstep.

The devastation in her face is gut wrenching. There aren't a whole lot of things that affect my soul anymore, but every time this woman is hurting, it sets my blood on fire.

I reach for her hand, then pull her over to me, cradling her between my legs, arms wrapped around her lightly. "We're going to figure this out. You know that, right?" I ask gently, giving her a reassuring squeeze.

"I don't know, Roman," she says, leaning her head back against my shoulder. An exasperated sigh leaves her lips, releasing the feeling of defeat into the air around us. That simply gesture has my heart aching. I want to fix it all, take away all the pain that she's gone through, along with all the pain that has yet to come from this fucked up situation. None of this is going to be easy or painless.

"I know it's overwhelming," I start, holding her securely against me still. "And it's okay to be scared about. Hell, I'd be a little worried if you weren't. This is real life with some real life consequences," I reassure. "But I'm not going anywhere, and we're going to figure it out. Together. Come hell or high water, I've got your back."

She wiggles into me, trying to get even a millimeter closer, seeking a comfort my words can't provide. All I can do for now is wait. Time will prove everything I've said to be true. Or not.

Fuck. How the fuck are we gonna get out of this? I think as her breathing slows and she starts to relax in my arms.

I press a quick kiss to the side of her head, rousing her from her sleepy state. "Sorry, sweetness. No time for naps today," I say as she protests, doubling down on staying warm and comfortable. She's so adorable when she's like this that it warms my heart just a little.

Stone cold heart turned to a pile of mush, I think, mentally chastising myself. *This is going to cause so much trouble.*

"Let's get some take out and watch a movie," I suggest, butterflies going wild in my stomach when her face lights up, bringing life back into her eyes for the first time today. "Your pick." I think she might explode from excitement at the thought.

"In pajamas?" she questions, one eyebrow raised, not daring get too excited. I nod and watch her come to life. The smile on her face could eclipse the sun, all troubles forgotten temporarily.

Shaking my head, I smile at her giddiness, content that I was able to bring this side back to light for an evening at least. As she leaps up and heads to the kitchen for the take-out menus, I pull out my phone, dread filtering back in as I pull up the contact.

I need your help. And your discretion.

I fire off the text before slipping my phone back into my pocket right as Jade comes bounding back into the room, menus in hand.

"I can't decide," she pouts, laying the menus out on the coffee table. "Everything sounds good."

"Who says we have to decide? Order whatever you want from wherever you want it from. We'll have it delivered and eat like kings tonight," I offer, shrugging.

"No way! That would be fun," she says, face still unsure. "We don't have to just pick one place?" she asks for confirmation.

"No, princess. Anything your heart desires, within my power, will be yours." The happiness returns just as my phone vibrates, threatening to pull a dark cloud over my evening with my sunshine girl. "You order. I'll pay," I say, pulling my card out of my back pocket, leaving my phone in place. She takes it hesitantly.

I kiss her forehead before heading for the bedroom. "Pajamas, remember?" I say, quelling the question on her face. When she returns her attention to the menus, I make my way to the bedroom and softly close the door behind me.

Do I even own pajamas? The shit I'm getting myself into for this girl. I think, shaking my head at the thought, even as the ever-present smile grows with the thought of her.

Pulling my phone from my back pocket, I unbutton my jeans and let them slide to the floor before stepping out of them. Opening the screen, I see a new text.

How can I help?

Breathing a huge sigh of relief, I shoot a text back, asking him to meet me here in a few hours. This isn't something I want to discuss over the phone or through text. This needs to be untraceable if it has any shot at all of working.

Pulling some old pajama pants from the closet, I slip them on, along with a ratty worn-out T-shirt, before heading back to the living room to find out the damages of our movie night at home.

Except the apartment is empty. The menus are still spread out over the coffee table, but Jade is nowhere to be found. Pulling up her name in my phone, I hit call and it immediately goes to her voicemail, instantly sending waves of panic through my system.

Slipping my shoes on, I pull open the front door and run straight into her, knocking both of us back a step.

"Are you okay?" she asks, registering the panic in my face. "I had to-" I pull her back inside and close the door before pressing into her, eliminating all space before my mouth covers hers, releasing the panic and rampant thoughts into the kiss.

After a moment of shock, she returns the kiss, fingers threading through my hair to keep me close. My hands on her hips, fingers digging into them in a punishing squeeze, my head starts to swim with desperation to be closer to her.

I bend and grip her thighs, wrapping her legs around my waist tightly. She doesn't break contact once, lost in the high of the connection.

A knock on the door pulls us back to reality, right as her back makes contact with the couch, my body hovering barely above hers. Her face is flushed, eyes heated. Pulling her lower lip in between her teeth, she wordlessly begs me to ignore the knock as it sounds again.

"Fuck," I say, barely above a whisper, nearly a growl. Pushing away from the couch, I'm devastated by the cold air, the warmth of her body leaving my skin.

"What do you need?" I demand through gritted teeth, opening the door to find a delivery guy with enough food to feed a small nation. Several bags in each hand, he looks up at me with nothing short of terror written across his face.

"My bad," I apologize, schooling my features to be more polite. "I wasn't expecting the food so quickly." Taking the bags from him, I thank him before heading for the kitchen, amusement clear in my face now. "You really couldn't decide, huh?" I laugh, placing the bags on the counter.

She blushes and I can't help but wonder if it's more from our moment being spoiled yet again or the proof of her indecision. She just shrugs, a smile plastered across her face still.

"I'm glad you ordered it all," I say, getting the food out and organized. "Now I won't have to go to the store for at least a week." She pushes my arm, sending me into full blown belly laughs. She's giggling now too, the sound soothing the gaping wound in my chest.

I wonder if this is what it feels like to be love-drunk. "Eat," I say, getting a plate out of the cabinet for each of us.

There are burgers, fries, milkshakes, chicken strips, salads. You name it, she ordered it. If I'm being honest, I might just make this a tradition. Not having to choose is quite nice.

When our plates are piled high with the fast food, we settle in on the couch, both sitting cross-legged with plates in our laps. Handing her the remote, I dig in while the food is still hot.

Without a moment of hesitation, she searches and finds our movie of the night. *Me Before You.* "I haven't seen this one before," I say as the intro starts up on the screen.

"It's my favorite. Besides *The Notebook* of course, but I wouldn't want to pick anything too girly or romantic, ya know." She shrugs, a sarcastic smile playing at her lips.

I give her another genuine smile before taking a bite of my burger and settling in. As the movie plays, I chase a thousand thoughts through my mind while trying to also pay attention. Mostly, I wonder what it is about this movie that really speaks to her.

As one of the main characters, Will, makes the insanely difficult decision to end his own suffering, I watch her face contort with the emotion warring inside her own head.

I'm not one to get all wrapped up in the emotions movies and books are supposed to pull from their audience, but I'll admit, this one has my heart aching. The simple thought of being put into that situation in my own life is enough to pull at my heartstrings.

For once, I'm rooting for true love to win. And in the end, as it so often does, true love triumphs – even if that means his life is over and the love of his life has to move on with hers. In the end, both lovers acted selflessly, giving every ounce of themselves to the other, even if that meant they couldn't be together from that point forward.

I see her swiping at her eyes as the credits begin to roll, making no attempt to cover her despair. She sighs dramatically, scrubbing her cheeks defiantly, as if that act will erase the aching in her chest.

It's in this moment I realize there are a million reasons to love this woman. There's not a single thing I wouldn't do for her, regardless of what that means for me or the rest of the human population.

Except one.

Chapter Twenty-Three

Roman

"Tell me your thoughts," she says excitedly, discarding her empty plate on the coffee table while turning her body to face me, eyes fixed on my face expectantly.

"You don't want to hear my thoughts," I laugh, brushing off the demand. My mind hasn't slowed down since the second I met this woman, let alone through this self-inflicted trauma scene disguised as a love story. Only a masochist watches this shit, I swear.

Her lower lips pops out, giving her the perfect pouty face. It's so cute I could die. Seeing her being so playful sets my blood on fire in a way I didn't know was possible.

So this is what being in love feels like, I think for the second time. The thought makes me queasy, but I'd be lying to myself if I didn't admit it also makes me a bit excited.

Rolling my eyes, I give in with a sigh. "Fine," I say, turning toward her now. "I think he was incredibly selfish." I press my forefinger against her lips to quiet her as she begins to protest my assessment. "I'm not finished," I continue, slightly raising my eyebrows.

She huffs but remains quiet as she crosses her arms over her chest, impatiently waiting for my explanation as if it's oxygen in a room deprived of air. Like my thoughts and feelings actually matter. *Fuck.*

"I think it was both incredibly selfish and self*less*," I press on. "He was in so much pain, both physically and mentally. It wasn't fair to himself to continue living in that condition. In that way, it was a very selfish decision to hurt everyone around him who loved him dearly in order to end his own suffering. Ensuring his pain would end but theirs would only be beginning."

Her eyes widen a fraction, taking in that perspective. She's frozen in place, waiting with bated breath.

"However, in the same instant, he was insanely selfless. He could have stayed, prevented Louisa's emotional pain, loved her for whatever time he had left." She nods, agreeing quietly, as if that's the only answer that makes any real sense. "But it was selfless to let her go."

"How do you figure?!" She's nearly frantic when the question spews from her lips. "He *left* her! Right after she had finally found happiness. And he was freaking happy with her!"

"You're absolutely right. I couldn't disagree if I tried. But she would have never gotten to experience the world if he had stayed. She would have stayed with him, taking care of him, never seeing the wonders the world has to offer. Never leaving that tiny town. She wouldn't have gotten the chance to authentically be herself. And that would have been too much guilt for him to bear," I finish, locking my gaze with her mesmerizing eyes.

"She never would have had a single complaint. She would have gladly given up anything in this world just to be with him," she pouts again, feeling passionately about these fictional people and their story. "She just wanted to be with him," she finished sadly, tears brimming again.

"Like I said, it was both selfish and selfless," I reiterate, taking her hand to pull her back into me, needing the warmth of her body pressed against mine again. I don't know how long we'll have together so I don't plan on wasting a single second of it.

"The good news is, neither of us have been in a terribly life-altering accident, so we're not going to have to make that decision," I remind her gently.

She sighs in contentment, taking solace in that truth, though what's to come may be more gruesome than any accident I could imagine.

***

Holding her flush against me in my bed, I begin to doze finally. We've been in bed for hours now, but my brain has refused to be quiet, keeping me awake as she sleeps peacefully next to me.

"Emily!" she screams, voiced pitched high in terror. She thrashes and pushes away from me, hands pulled into tight fists. Her face is contorted in the dim light, showing a strange mix of fear and anger.

I reach for her, barely grazing her arm when she begins to wail, releasing unbridled grief and panic. Her eyes are still closed, still entirely asleep as the nightmare wreaks havoc on her mentally.

"Jade," I say gently, reaching out to run my fingertips down her cheek, hoping a light touch will bring her out of the nightmare and back to reality where I can keep her safe. "Jade, baby, you're having a nightmare but I'm right here. Wake up for me, darling," I coax gently, her eyes fluttering as she fights to regain consciousness.

It takes several more seconds before her eyes fully open, coated with sleep and confusion. They widen in a panic before she sits bolt upright in the bed, sweat sliding down her forehead, down her cheeks and neck before disappearing into the cloth of my t-shirt she had donned before crawling into bed with me. The sight makes my stomach do somersaults.

As her breathing gradually slows, her shoulders drop and the tension bleeds out of her body. She slides back down, laying back down again, though she lays a little way away from me now. Turning on her side, her gaze finds mine. Her eyes still look sleepy, even though she's fighting it now, afraid to return to that hell.

"I never sleep anymore," she says, sadness flitting through her eyes and into her voice. "Not since everything happened. I have that same nightmare damn near every night. It's killing me from the inside out," she confesses, frustration seeping into her voice to mingle with the sadness that remains there.

"I'm right here," I say, reaching out to stroke her hair away from her face. "I'll be here to fight those demons with you. And if I can't figure out how to fight them, I'll at least sit with you in the dark." The promise brings a small smile to her lips but the grief remains in her eyes.

My phone buzzes on the nightstand, drawing my attention away. Rolling over, I reach for it and find a text.

On my way. Got caught up.

Fuck. I completely forgot.

I lock the screen, blanketing us in darkness again, minus the small table lamp on the nightstand.

"I have something I need to take care of," I explain, tossing the cover off my legs and swinging them over the side of the bed. "Try to get some rest and I'll be back in a little bit." I lean down to kiss her forehead as she protests.

"I'm not saying you can't come with me," I offer. "I just wanted to let you know I'm going to be up for a while still in case you wanted to get some shut eye in the meantime." Before the words are out of my mouth, she's tossing back the cover and planting both feet on the floor.

"I suggest throwing on a pair of pants then," I say, looking her up and down as a fire grows in the pit of my stomach. She looks damn fine standing on the other side of the bed in just my t-shirt, hair just a little messy from our time spent lounging in the bed. I feel the heat reach my face as she pulls her bottom lip between her teeth, a similar heat making its way to her eyes as they unapologetically take in my shirtless chest.

I move to the closet, away from her, before I can't contain myself and ruin the whole meeting I need to attend to. Finding a pair of plaid pajama pants, I toss them to her before I can change my mind. I can't look away as she slowly steps into them, pulling them up to sit loosely on her waist.

Nodding, I head for the kitchen to make a pot of coffee. I'm going to need it to get through this, but this is necessary.

Less than five minutes pass before there's a sharp knock on the door. Flipping the deadbolt back, I open the door and turn back toward the living room without even looking at our guest.

"Thanks for coming," I say, turning to greet him with a cup of coffee in hand. He takes it, nodding his thanks.

"Anytime," he says, taking a barstool at the island. "What's so important?"

"I need a favor. A big one, Finn," I say honestly. Finn has been by my side since day one. James wasn't super keen on taking me in, especially after I fucked up the first assignment he had given me.

It was a simple order. Track down a local crackhead who owed James some money. Bring him in. When James was finished with him, return the guy to whatever shithole I happened to have found him in. Easy. Except I fucked up.

Everything had gone as smoothly as you could hope for until the drop off. I was watching every step, keeping an eye on every person around. The stakes were high for me on this one. One fuck up and it could get me killed. Or any of us really.

I didn't see the guy watching me from the second story of the run-down apartment building where I had originally found this guy.

Unfortunately for me, this wasn't just any guy. The creeper was from a rival group, and the target owed money to them as well. They hadn't been able to find him until I led them straight to his fucking doorstep.

Luckily, I got the sense that something wasn't quite right, though I couldn't pinpoint what it was, and switched things up on my way back out. I didn't go straight home, didn't go back to the warehouse office. Turns out, that bit of trusting my gut saved my life.

If that guy hadn't killed me, James would have done it in a heartbeat. A fuck up like that can get everybody killed. Being discreet is quite literally a matter of life and death in this business.

The morning after the drop off, there was a knock on the warehouse door. Darting my eyes between James and the door, I held my breath, being deadly quiet. As the door squeaked open, I could see a small package on the step. Just a plain cardboard box but packaged neatly with James's name scrawled across the top.

James didn't bother to bring it inside, opening it right there on the step. Trying to look around him without invading his space, I caught a glimpse of red around his shoulder. He picked up the box, stepped inside, and used his foot to close the steel door. The thud as the door came fully to was sickening.

James placed the small box on the table to the right of the door, opening it fully and giving me a knowing look. I stepped forward, already feeling nauseous without even seeing the contents.

This is bad, I thought instinctively. *This is really bad.*

Peeking into the box, all I can see at first is red. There's red everywhere. In the center of the box, cradled delicately in newspaper wrapping, is a hand. A human fucking hand.

My eyes dart nervously to James's face, finding no sympathy there. Just a look of anger. Hatred almost. There was no pity, no understanding.

Without the words being spoken aloud, I knew with a sickening clarity that I had gotten this man killed last night. I wasn't careful enough and it cost this poor guy his life.

I do my best to keep on my feet, keeping my legs under me through sheer willpower. "Fuck" was all I could manage. My throat felt as dry as the desert.

James turned without a word, leaving the present lying on the dirty table for any passerby to see. He wanted the guys here to know I fucked up. To know they couldn't trust me.

I stared at the box for a long while, completely unseeing and unaware of anything going on around me. People came and went. Harsh looks thrown my way, though none affected me like the look I'd seen on James's face. That one gutted me.

Shortly after, I heard shouting from the office before Finn emerged, a small pity smile on his face. With a simple nod, he descended the steps and left the warehouse for whatever assignment he'd been on that day. Within seconds, James had stepped out onto the landing, looked me dead in the eye, then turned and went back to his desk, leaving the door open with a silent command.

I took the steps one at a time, praying I would get to see the dirty warehouse floor at the bottom at least one more time. I wasn't sure what he could want, but I did know it couldn't possibly be good. Not after this morning.

Fuck, I was half tempted to jump off the landing before even setting foot in his office just to end the anxiety that was welling up in my chest, making it harder to breathe the closer I got to that office door.

"Yes, sir?" I said, poking my head around the side of the door.

He had a desk lamp on, shrouding the rest of the room in a dim light. It cast harsh shadows over his face, making him look ten times more deadly than he did on a regular day, which I had thought would be impossible up until that point. I'd be lying if I said I wasn't terrified as I peeked into the office that day.

He didn't reply, waiting for me to have the balls to step in fully. With a deep breath, I stepped through the threshold, terrified but willing to accept whatever was coming my way.

"Close the door," he said, keeping his eyes trained on the open laptop in front of him.

When I did, he motioned to the worn out leather seats in front of him. I took a seat, scooted all the way to the edge.

He turned the laptop to me slowly. On the screen there was a picture of three small children. Two little girls and an infant boy. They were smiling and happy, eyes full of life. He clicked the arrow, scrolling to a second picture. A beautiful woman, dark auburn hair with green eyes, standing beside a young man who was holding her swollen stomach.

I swallowed the bile down as it rose in my throat. It was the man I had dropped off last night.

"He had a family," I say with finality, using the past tense intentionally. James wouldn't be showing me this if this man was still alive.

"He did," he says, letting the pause hang in the air between us. "The things we do here matter. They have consequences. A lot of times, those consequences are the difference between life and death, Roman. You cost this man his life. Those children no longer have a father because you were careless." The gravity of the situation presses down on my shoulder, making it difficult to pull a full breath into my lungs.

"I can't have that kind of carelessness here on my team," he continued, turning the computer back to face him again. "We *can't* fuck up here."

"I know. Fuck, I know. I saw the guy watching from the second floor. I just didn't know he was part of another team for sure," I say as an explanation, not as an excuse. No excuse is going to fix this. "Excuse me," I say, standing while I still have the strength left to do so.

"Wait." Instantly, I stop, halfway to standing out of the chair. Lowering myself slowly back into the chair, I do my best to reign in the panic building in my blood as he closes the laptop lid.

"I'll be completely honest with you, Roman," he began, lacing his fingers together on the wooden desk in front of him. "I wasn't excited about bringing you into this. I don't think you're built for it. Your heart is too soft. But I brought you in anyway, hoping you could hack it. This whole instance has proven me right the way I see it. Your oversight cost this man his life." He pauses, weighing my reaction.

I do my best to keep my features neutral, though a wave of despair and anger are rushing over me simultaneously, threatening to drown me in my own head. I remain still, unfazed.

"Unfortunately, Finn sees potential in you," he continues. "He's been my right-hand man for years now. His story isn't too different from yours. You'd do good to ask him about it sometime. But anyway, he pointed out that you were careful. You covered your tracks. Took different paths in and out. Tracked the guy down with no assistance from anyone here.

"You're resourceful and your responses are appropriate. You think for yourself instead of falling into line with everyone else without reason. I like that in my men." He stretches his arms above his head, leaning back in his seat, cupping the back of his neck.

"With that being said, against my better judgement, I'm going to give you another shot. With some additional training. You'll be with Finn for the next couple weeks, learning everything he can teach you about what we do here. The good and the bad. If, at the end of that time, he still thinks you have potential, you're welcome to stay." His face looks tense as he finishes, like it's physically painful for him to say the words.

I'll have to remember how important Finn is here. That could be useful in the future.

Over the next few weeks, my skills improved significantly. Finn and I spent time at the shooting range, scouring the internet for information using different techniques to stay hidden, and scouting the areas we had control over. I learned so much from him in that short time and truly felt like I had finally found where I belonged. I was made for this job. Until she came along.

Chapter Twenty-Four

Jade

Stretching my sleep taut muscles, I take his suggestion and snag a pair of sleep pants from his closet. Pulling them over my feet quickly, I do my best to keep up with him as he heads for the living room.

"Hey," I say behind him, finally tugging the pants up to my waist. "What's this all about?"

"I told you I had a plan," he starts, turning so abruptly that I damn near run into his chest. "Finn is on his way here so we can get started on it. That's what I'm hoping for at least. I'm not sure how he's going to feel about everything considering what happened with James."

As if on cue, there's a light knock on the door announcing his arrival. Roman clicks back the deadbolt, opening the door for him. "Thanks for coming, Finn," he says, stepping back to allow him inside.

"What's this all about, Roman?" Finn asks, not making any time for pleasantries. "I know it can't be good if you got yourself kicked out of the warehouse and need a favor right after."

Roman gives him a simple nod before leading him into the living room and offering him a seat. "Let's get right to it then, shall we?" he asks, situating himself across from where Finn now sits, perched on the edge of the chair. "I went to James to ask for help. He obviously turned me down, given the details I'm about to share with you. I'll understand if you do the same, but I could really use somebody I can trust in my corner."

Ten minutes later, after spewing out all the details yet again, Finn leans back into the chair. "I don't know, man," he begins, scrubbing a hand through his hair. "Why not just hand me a pen so I can sign my own death warrant?" A deep, gravelly chuckles leaves him but there's no real amusement in it.

"I know it's a lot. I wouldn't ask if I had any other option," Roman explains, fully aware that if we can't get Finn's help, we're absolutely fucked. The only option left is to run and live the rest of my life looking over my shoulder, hoping the cops don't catch up and Cain decides to just let it go eventually, which doesn't seem likely.

Finn is quite a bit shorter than Roman, standing about 5'10" if I was guessing. He looks like a completely different man than when I first met him now. He's freshly showered, hair a little shaggy, and no longer smells of stale cigarettes. Truthfully, he's a painfully handsome man when he's cleaned up a bit.

Roman had told me he had been on a mission right before I met him. Apparently that's how a lot of them go. No showers, almost homeless appearances to fit in. Sometimes working for days with no breaks to clean up or even sleep more than a few minutes at a time. I shiver at the memory of that conversation and the ones that followed. The conversations about his hardest tasks along the way, though he spared me most of the gory details thankfully.

Turning to me, Finn scoots back to the edge of his seat, gaze locking with mine. I find myself unable to look away, mesmerized by the deep shades of green I find there. "I've never known Roman to go so far to protect anyone," he starts, holding the contact for a few moments longer. "Fucking hell," he says on a sigh, shaking his head lightly.

"Are you in or what?" Roman asks, starting to lose patience.

"You know I'm in, fucker," Finn says, rolling his eyes for dramatic effect. "I'm always in. I've got a thing for beating the odds," he says, winking at me with a smile.

"Wait. In for what exactly?" I ask, eyes darting between the two of them. I'm sitting in a room with literal killers and I've never felt safer in my life, even if one misstep could get us all killed or imprisoned.

"The plan," Roman says. "We're going to get this shit figured out and get the cops off your back. Permanently. Nobody's every going to find out what actually happened to Emily or the part you played in it."

"Fuck," I say, tears pricking my eyes as my throat starts to burn. "Thank you, Finn. And you too." A single tear slides down my cheek before I'm scrubbing them away, determined to keep it together for now.

"I'll call Sara first thing in the morning," Roman says, turning his attention back to Finn. "I need her to check in on the situation with the cops. Get us an update there. You come in after that. I'll let you know when I get word back from her and we'll initiate the plan then."

"Sounds good, brother," Finn says, standing from the chair and smoothing out his jeans. "I'll be waiting."

"Thanks for everything," Roman says, sincerity bleeding from him. "I appreciate you more than you know."

"Just don't get me fucking killed," he responds with a smile. "I've still got women left to worship." With a wink back at me, he makes his way to the door, and after a quick goodbye, he's out the door, leaving me feeling like I can actually breathe again.

Roman scrubs his hand down his face, now dotted with new stubble, before turning his attention back to me.

"Well. Good news, believe it or not," he says, eyes coming back to life again. "Finn did some digging and it doesn't seem like Cain has any real interest in coming after you. It honestly doesn't seem like the debt Emily owed him really meant anything to him." He shrugs, putting me a little more at ease.

"That is good. I'm surprised," I admit. "It seems like this world is all about money and nothing else makes a fuck." I pinch the bridge of my nose, hoping to fight off the oncoming headache.

"It is. But I'm guessing she really didn't owe him that much. He's got bigger fish to fry. Plus, she sold her body to him and his men several times from what I've been hearing. A lot of these guys are willing to let go of a small debt for that exchange." The look of disgust that crosses his face has my stomach doing flips.

"One demon down, then," I say, forcing a small smile. It doesn't feel like much of a victory, but I'll take anything I can get at this point. Plus, having Finn on our side is a major bonus. As long as we can keep that information quiet, that is.

"It's all gonna be alright," he says, reading my face. I've really got to work on that poker face.

"I know," I say, actually believing it for the first time since I started having the nightmares and realized what I'd done.

"Good. Now... where were we?" he asks, giving me a wicked half smile that could melt the coldest of hearts.

"Hmm. I believe we were at the part where we snuggle up and forget about the crazy world we've managed to dive into," I say, stretching as a yawn overtakes me.

"No, no," he says, leaning forward to get closer to my face, eyes darting between my eyes and lips. "Before that."

"You'll have to refresh my memory I guess," I say, shrugging as a smile tugs on my lips. "I seem to have forgotten."

He chuckles darkly before covering my mouth with his again, sliding his hand around to cup the back of my neck, fingers reaching up into my hair. A soft moan escapes me before I can help it, lost in the kiss.

He nips my bottom lip before running his tongue over it gently. When I open to him, his tongue enters my mouth smoothly, exploring every inch. My hands are roaming his shoulders, committing every muscle to memory.

His free hand runs up and down my side before sliding gently under the t-shirt I swiped from him earlier. The feel of his skin on mine has goosebumps popping up anywhere he touches, evidence of the effect he has on me. That has him smiling into the kiss now, sending my heart into overdrive.

As quickly as it started, it's over and Roman is pushing himself up, away from me. The separation leaves me feeling hollow and cold. Just as I'm about to play it off, feigning indifference, he reaches for me, pulling me to my feet before hoisting me up to wrap my legs around his waist.

His kiss is different when it comes again moments later. He slowly walked us to the bedroom, laying me gently onto the king size bed before standing to his full height, looking me head to toe with a dark hunger in his eyes.

Crawling up to meet me on the bed, the energy shifts as he covers my body with his this time. Up until now, it's all been flirting and games. His lips meet mine, hungry and lust-filled, as his bruising kiss steals my breath. I'm panting by the time he lets up to trace my jaw with his lips.

Down to my neck, to that sweet soft spot where my neck meets my shoulder, where the flesh is so tender. He nips at it with his teeth, releasing a moan from deep within my chest. When he bites again, this time harder, my back arches from the bed, both in pain and a surprising pleasure. Heat and tension are already building in my core at the simple act.

I run my fingers through his hair, tugging at it lightly. The sensation is too much as he nips the skin on my neck over and over, following it by kissing and licking the assaulted skin. Curling my fingers into his hair, I pull harder, trying to pry him away from the sensitive spot.

Quicker than I can comprehend, both of my wrists are pinned above my head in one of his hands. A squeal escapes my lips, much to his amusement. The smug grin has me melting on the inside and wriggling on the outside.

It's no use, though. He's stronger than me, no matter how hard I fight against his hold.

Thankfully, he moves his lips slowly from my neck to my collar bone, lightly running his tongue over the skin there. Suddenly, I have no fight left in me.

"Good girl," he whispers as he moves back up to graze the shell of my ear with his lips. A shudder racks my body, goosebumps reappearing the second the praise leaves his mouth.

He releases my wrists long enough to peel my shirt from my body, careful not to tangle my hair in it. Tossing it to the floor, his eyes slowly devour my exposed body, flames building in them.

Suddenly too aware that I have no clue what to do with my hands, I thread my fingers back into his hair and pull his body back down to mine, desperate to close the distance between us.

One hand supporting his weight, the other roaming my body, it feels like he touches me gently for hours, caressing every bare inch of my skin, following the touches with quick kisses. My breath hitches as he slips a finger under the waistband of the pajama pants I stole from him. Slowly pulling them down my legs, I feel the cool air hit my skin.

Sliding his hand firmly from my calf all the way back up to my hip, the energy shifts from slow and sensual to hungry and impatient. He makes quick work of my bra, discarding it on the floor with the other forgotten clothes, all while taking in the sight of my breasts, nipples peaked from the exposure and cool air.

Covering one with his hand, squeezing gently, he pulls the other nipple into his mouth, expertly swirling his tongue around it. A gasp escapes me, not quite expecting it to feel that fucking good.

I yelp when he nips the sensitive bud, immediately soothing it with his tongue after. I've always enjoyed a little pain with sex, but the pleasure of having the pain kissed or licked away is a whole new thing that has me squeezing my thighs together to abate the pressure building between them.

Kissing down my stomach, Roman makes his way to my hips, making sure to kiss each one before sliding his hand over my center. The brush of his fingers over the thin material of my panties nearly sends me over the edge.

My breath is ragged as he pulls the material aside, getting a full view. The hunger in his eyes is astonishing.

He kisses down my left thigh to my knee, then back up, following the same pattern on the other leg before spreading them wider. He kisses each inner thigh, so close to my center, before nipping the skin, inciting another low moan.

One quick move and the panties are gone, torn away from my body. I feel my face begin to flush, heat rising to my cheeks as he takes his time running his fingers up and down my inner thigh. When I feel like I might explode from anticipation, he finally touches me, rubbing slow circles around my clit.

That simple touch sends fireworks through my veins, pulling me right to the edge within seconds. I'm fighting for my life as he sinks a finger inside me. His thumb finds its way back to my clit, circling it with a steady pressure that sends me careening over the edge in seconds.

"Good girl," he praises, keeping his pace until the high begins to taper off. Placing one hand on his forearm, I try to pull him back up toward me. "No, ma'am. I didn't say I was finished with you yet."

A chill racks my body at his words and the confidence oozing from him. He smirks before sliding down the bed to lay on his stomach. Sniper position. Hooking both arms around my thighs, he inhales with a groan before locking his gaze with mine. Eyes locked, he kisses my thighs agonizingly slowly before following suit with my center. Slow kisses down, then back up again. I'm damn near shaking with anticipation.

Flattening his tongue, he licks me from top to bottom and back again, taking his time. A moan comes from me as a low rumbling groan vibrates through my pussy from him. When his tongue finds my clit, circling it over and over, I nearly come undone. I can feel the beginnings of an orgasm building in my core, no matter how I try to fight it off. It feels too damn good.

One hand finds its way to each side of his head, fingers entangled in his hair as he laps me up. Closer and closer to falling off that edge with every movement, his name slips from my lips like a prayer.

"That's right, baby. Pray to me while I worship you," he says against my core. He slips one finger inside me, followed quickly by another. The full feeling has me teetering on the edge, destined to come apart at the seams.

"Fuck," I say, voice breathy and heated. "Fuck, fuck, fuck." The more I say it, the quicker his movements become, both of us now chasing the impending orgasm.

Pulling my clit into his mouth, he sucks gently, forcing me to explode around him yet again. My back arches from the bed, hands gripping his head tighter in an attempt to stay tethered to earth somehow as I hit that climax.

"You look so pretty when you come for me, baby," he praises, fueling me further.

Eventually, I start to come back down as his movements slow. He smirks up at me before making his way back up the bed. Wiping my come from his face, he kisses me deeply, leaving me breathless for the millionth time tonight.

I wrap my hand around him as he kisses me, finding him already hard. He bites my lip, groaning into the kiss as I run my hand up and down his shaft. My lip slips from his teeth as I move to straddle his legs.

One hand on his hip, the other still wrapped around him, I take his smooth head into my mouth, swirling my tongue around it. Locking eyes with him as the first *fuck* falls from his lips, I pull more of him into my mouth, loving the thrill running through my body at the sounds he makes with every movement of my tongue.

Moving my hand away, I take him entirely in my mouth and quickly down my throat, causing him to thread his fingers through my hair. I grip his balls lightly in one hand as I take him in my throat again, living for the curses under his breath.

He gives me no more than three minutes before he's tugging my hair roughly, pulling me up off of him as his dick pulses underneath my tongue, so close to the edge. Using my thumb to wipe the side of my mouth as I pull my lower lip between my teeth, I admire the animal I can see behind his eyes. He's all predator inside.

He pulls me up to straddle his hips, moving me over his dick but not going any farther, allowing me to take my time now. He lines up with my center, both dying for a release but wanting it to last forever.

I ease down onto him, taking just the tip with a gasp. Moving up and down tantalizingly slowly, I take more of him, inch by inch, until he's seated deep inside me. "Fuck," I say again, amazed at the feeling. He's stretched me to the point of bordering on pain, yet still feels incredible.

Slowly, I move up and down, adjusting to his width as well as length. It takes several minutes of slow movements to accommodate myself, but the pleasure takes over soon as I ride him.

His hands on my hips, he sets the pace while allowing me to move in whatever way feels best for me. "God, you look incredible," he says, eyes lust-filled.

"You *feel* incredible," I fire back, relishing the feeling of him as it leaves me breathless. Every movement hits a different spot, all of them bringing me closer to tumbling over the edge. It feels like every nerve in my body is on fire.

Before I'm able to comprehend what's happening, I'm on my back with Roman above me. Legs wrapped around him, he slowly enters me again. Kissing me deeply once again, his fingers pressing into my hips as he thrusts into me.

Leaning back, he takes one leg in each hand, placing my feet on his shoulders as he picks up his pace, effectively taking my breath.

"Fuck," he groans, doing his best to keep steady. "Come with me," he demands, hips stuttering as he fights his release, waiting for me.

That simple command sends me into a spiral. I come undone around him as he pumps into me a final time, following me over the edge.

Rolling to the side, he collapses beside me, breathing heavily. His eyes are hooded with exhaustion now but he looks completely satisfied as he runs his fingertips up and down my stomach slowly. It was in that tender moment I knew things would never be the same. There was no going back.

253

Chapter Twenty-Five

Roman

I got the info you asked for.

Scrubbing my eyes and squinting against the harsh light, I reread the message from Sara. I had messaged her last night to see what she could come up with as far as the police's developments on our case.

Groaning, I slide my arm out from under Jade's still sleeping body. Grinning as I look down at her finally looking at peace, I force myself up off the bed. If I keep looking at her, I'll end up right back beside her, the world outside be damned.

Unfortunately, there's too much at stake here. *She's* at stake here to be exact. And as much as I'd love to lounge around with her, I have to be proactive at keeping this whole mess at bay until we can start working on our plan to move forward.

After looking through a bit more of Emily's texts with Cain last night, we discovered that the situation was actually far worse than we had originally thought. We knew she had mentioned trading Jade as payment when her body failed to pay off the debt in full. What we didn't know was Emily had already set that in motion by giving him Jade's information and helping him make a plan to abduct her. A plan Emily had full intentions of being involved in.

She was going to tell Jade they were going to swing by a friend's house on the way to their regular Saturday evening dinner. They went to dinner every other Saturday for a girl's night out, so this wouldn't have raised any red flags.

At this friend's house, everything would seem normal. Emily would hand over some cash for some 'makeup', hug, say their goodbyes, and head out to dinner. In reality, the whole thing was a charade. It would allow Cain to get a look at Jade, mentally note what she was wearing, and catalog that for later when he would spike her drink at dinner.

Jade would ask to leave due to not feeling so well. Emily, the ever-concerned best friend would help her outside where a group of Cain's men would be waiting next to her car.

They would grab her, and we all know the rest of the story from there. It's a gruesome one at best.

The fact that Emily had made this plan herself with full intention to participate made it that much more repulsive. The shit Cain does, what all the men in this world do, is bad enough on its own without involving people who are supposed to have your back.

With that being said, we now had a potentially bigger problem than the police. If he had all that information at hand, deal already made, there's nothing to say he wouldn't try to take Jade regardless of the fact that Emily was dead and the debt should've been wiped clean the second she stopped breathing.

"Talk to me," I say as soon as she answers. Sara's normally calm voice has an eerie edge to it when she speaks. It sends sparks of electricity through my veins as each word passes her lips.

"I've been up all night trying to get some answers," she yawns. "It's not good news, but not the worst I've ever delivered either. Not by a long shot." She pauses with that, no doubt cycling through the memories of the times that have been worse news. "Anyway. The cops aren't too far off from figuring it out. They've got the video but haven't been able to piece together the part that was cut. They've also tried to get Emily's phone records but haven't been able to persuade the phone company just yet. Apparently, they don't know how to sweet talk," she says, a smile evident in her voice.

I chuckle at that. Sara's definitely a smooth talker when she needs to be. I'm beyond thankful to Patty for putting me in touch with her. She's been extremely valuable to have on my side. Hopefully she still feels the same when she finds out the full truth about Jade and the new direction we're heading.

"That's not terrible news," I start, breathing a hesitant sigh of relief. At least one problem off my shoulders for right now. "What about the rest?"

"Ah. That's where the 'not good' news come into play," she begins, taking her time. "Cain is a terrible fuck. Like God awful waste of space kind of human. Do you know some of the shit he's done?! It's literally insane. He makes Bundy look like a nice guy." I close my eyes, pinching the bridge of my nose. I know the guy. Fuck, I helped train the guy before he decided to go at it on his own when James felt he was out of control.

"I do. Continue please." My patience is already wearing thin this morning.

"Alright, alright. So the best I can figure, he's still interested in taking her. I haven't seen anything definite of course. They're not going to say that right out in a text. But there's been a few texts that would cause me to think she's not out of danger when it comes to him." As she relays the information, I can feel the tension building in the back of my neck. Pent up frustration from the past few weeks ready to boil over.

"Keep tabs on him for me? Let me know if anything interesting pops up. And Sara? We need to meet up this afternoon. There's been some changes that need to be discussed. Meet me here sometime after 6 this evening." Without waiting for a response, I hang up the phone and slip it back into my pocket.

Exhaustion racks my body as I push up from my seat on the couch and head to the kitchen, needing some caffeine if I'm going to have any chance of making it through the day.

Just as I push the start button on the machine, Jade shuffles around the corner, looking adorably disheveled. Even with her hair a mess and makeup smudged around her eyes from yesterday, she's the most beautiful thing I've ever laid eyes on.

"Good morning, sleeping beauty. How'd you sleep?" I ask, smiling at her as she holds out her arms and walks straight into my chest before wrapping them tightly around me. I kiss the top of her head as she sighs against me, sounding content.

"I slept like a rock," she laughs, looking up at me with half-asleep eyes. "I haven't slept that good in years. Maybe ever. How about you?"

"I slept really well," I admit, relishing the feel of her in my arms again. "It was nice to finally have you here with me for the whole night."

Her entire face lights up before a blush creeps into her cheeks and has her hiding her face against me. I love that she wears her feelings on her sleeve. I just hope that doesn't cause a problem for us as we navigate through all of this.

"Sara is coming over tonight. I'm going to tell her the truth about us and why you killed Emily," I say, holding up a hand when she tries to protest. "She needs to know. She's been my biggest help since I started working on this entire thing. If I don't tell her, and she finds out some other way, she could ruin our future before it even has a chance to get started. I'm not willing to risk that with you."

Instead of arguing, she simply nods, pulling her lip between her teeth to pick at the skin there. I've noticed it's a nervous habit of hers lately.

"I think she'll understand once everything is laid out," I say honestly. I can't be 100% certain, and I was wrong about James, but I'd bet Sara is more logically driven than emotionally driven. She gets off on obtaining the facts and making sense of them.

The entire day is spent relaxing, just enjoying each other's company. Chinese take-out for lunch. A cheesy romantic sap story on tv. Cuddling and intimate conversation. Literally a dream. But every dream is short-lived.

A knock on the door wakes us both from this dream we've been living all day. Back to reality. The weight is nearly soul-crushing as I make my way to the door, knowing this could be the end of everything I've ever wanted. The only shot at happiness I've ever had.

"Sara," I greet her, opening the door wide to let her through.

"You said we needed to talk?" she says, slipping off her shoes by the door before heading to the living room. She stops cold several feet from the room, dead in her tracks. Turning, she stares at me with confusion written across her face. Maybe a little anger also.

It's obvious she interrupted something intimate here. Two lovers spending quality time together, both still dressed in pajamas regardless of the hour.

"I think you know Jade," I start, motioning for her to pick a seat.

"Kind of, yes," she stammers, still processing what she's stumbled into.

"Hear me out," I say, taking the seat beside Jade again. She's shrunk back into the couch, trying her best to be invisible. "There's a lot you don't know. A lot I didn't really understand when we found that video."

"Right," Sara says quietly, taking a seat in the chair on the other side of the coffee table to face us.

Jade and I tell her the whole story, sparing no details about that night and everything that led up to it. By the end, tears are streaming down Jade's face and Sara still doesn't look entirely sold on the story.

"I know it's hard to believe," Jade says, sniffling and wiping at her nose with a tissue. "But I can show you the texts.

Show you everything she had been saying to all these people. All the plans she had made to fucking *sell* me to them."

"No need," Sara says, more calm now than she has been since she walked through the door. "You've been through a lot already. No need to keep bringing all of that back into your life."

"We need your help," I level with her. "I'm no good with the police. I've never had any real dealings with the legal side of this shit. Only what's done in the dark."

"I don't do super well with the police, Roman. But I think I can plant some things in the video that might help steer them into a different direction. Eventually, they're going to recover the deleted parts of the video. I can't prevent that. But maybe I can tweak it a bit." She pulls out her phone, types out a text, then places it back into her jacket pocket.

"Thank you," Jade begins. "So much. You have no idea how much I appreciate you."

"It's no big deal. The police would never believe you. Even with the evidence right there in front of them, they'd still try to convict you on her murder just so they could put someone away for it," Sara reasons, seeming more comfortable now that everything is out on the table.

"Thank you for everything you've done," I say, hoping the sincerity bleeds through into my voice. "The only other issue at the moment is Cain and keeping an eye on him. I don't want him getting anywhere close to her, and I'd be lying if I said I thought this was all over just because Emily is dead."

Sara stiffens in her seat again, looking between us before locking her gaze with mine. "You absolutely should still be concerned about him. The man is a total fuckhead. I've got access to his phone, as well as a couple of guys who are working with him. Nothing damning has come across them so far, but he knows better than to send anything like that."

As she stands to leave, she straightens her jacket before looking between us again. "I sincerely wish you both the best. I'll be in touch if I hear anything worth sharing."

I walk her to the door, closing it softly behind her before exhaling a lungful of air, feeling my mood deflate right along with my chest.

Doing my best to keep the mood light, I turn back to find Jade staring at the coffee table, ignoring me completely. "You okay?" I ask, snagging a bottle of water from the fridge before rejoining her in the living room.

"Yeah," she says blandly. "Totally okay." The sarcasm dripping from her voice is a little much, but I totally get it. The last few days have been a lot to take in. Hell, the last several weeks have been a lot.

"Hey," I say, sitting down and nudging her shoulder with mine while offering a small smile. "It's all going to be just fine. You heard Sara. She's going to help with the video footage to the police. That's a major win for us. That should hopefully get them onto a different track and buy us some time."

"Yeah, I heard that. What wasn't convincing was the conversation around the 'fuckhead' who was trying to buy me. The conversation that turns my stomach to lead any time his name is brought up," she says, gaze locking with mine. The look in her eye is not anything close to what it's been lately. This is more like... giving up.

"We've got this. Even if he does come for you, we'll figure it out and never let that happen," I soothe, rubbing her thigh gently. "Besides, I trained the fuckhead so I think I probably have a few tricks left up my sleeve that I forgot to teach him," I shrug.

The look of shock that crosses her face would almost be laughable if we were in any situation other than the one we're currently facing.

I may have taught Cain a lot of what he knows, but we differ in one major way. I have a moral compass I tend to follow. He doesn't. That's the biggest thing that makes him so damn dangerous, especially in a situation like this one.

He'll go to the ends of the earth to get what he feels is his. Even if that's a woman I've fallen madly in love with.

Chapter Twenty-Six

Jade

The chill that comes over my body from finding out Roman trained Cain is unlike anything I've experienced before. It's like I was instantly frozen from the inside out. Breath and blood stopping as I tried to process what just came out of his mouth.

"I trained him years ago," he explains quickly. "When he first got into this lifestyle, I was assigned to train him and keep him from dying. After about a year, he started to worry me. I talked to James, but he did nothing." He looks sorrowful as he fills me in on his history with Cain.

"He started doing some fucked up shit. Taking children, holding them hostage and demanding ransom. When the mothers didn't have the cash to get their kid back, he would kindly offer them other 'payment options'. That went against everything we were doing." There's a fury bubbling underneath the calm he's trying to maintain.

"I went back to James about it, and he actually listened this time. The conversation between the two was pretty heated. All I know is Cain stormed out of James's office, slamming the door behind him, all while telling James to go fuck himself," he finishes, letting me absorb the information.

"That's a lot," I finally say, at a loss for any other words still.

"It is. I hadn't heard much about him since then. A few run-ins with guys he's employed through the last few years. A couple rumors of some terrible things he's done, though I never bothered to dig into it and find out if any of that was even true. Now I wish I had kept up with him more. Maybe learned how he's been operating since he left," he says, running his hand through his hair.

For the first time, I notice the dark circles under his eyes. He looks like he hasn't had a good night's sleep in a decade, which probably isn't far from the truth. I'd imagine it'd be hard to sleep well with all that on your conscience.

"We'll get through it, remember?" I say, repeating his words to me. Even as unsure as I am, it helps to have him being confident about that, so I push through my discomfort and try to make it sound as positive as possible. Like it's an undeniable truth.

***

The next week is unremarkable. Dinner dates, movie nights, mind-blowing sex, and future plans. It's a whirlwind that has me gasping for breath, but I'm loving every single second of it.

Very little of our time is spent apart now. Mostly just when I have some writing to get done and he needs to finish some editing, though we sometimes do that together as well.

In all the bliss, I've managed to nearly forget all the danger looming around us, ready to take us out at any second. I've forgotten to be constantly aware of my surroundings and have drifted back toward my old care-free lifestyle without a second thought. Even Roman seems to have let his guard down some.

Until today that is.

Exactly one week from our last conversation with Sara, where things felt so settled. Our last night of deep discussions about dark possibilities that may be being reality in the coming days.

As I made my way to my front door after an hour at the gym this afternoon, a creeping feeling washed over me. Almost like I was being watched. I shook it off as best I could until I actually got to my front door, unlocked it, slid inside, and quietly shut and locked it behind me.

As soon as I turned my back to the door, panic slid over me like a blanket, coating my every nerve ending. The hair on my arms rose, along with the hair on the back of my neck. I was coated in goosebumps as I silently tiptoed into my apartment.

Nothing seemed out of place. Everything was exactly where I had left it. As I breathed a sigh of relief, determined to shake whatever paranoia this was, I noticed it.

A single piece of paper stuck to my fridge. Scrawled across it, a note is written in sloppy handwriting. Written in a hurry. But the bottom of the page is what causes my stomach to somersault, sending my heartrate through the roof.

Hello, precious.
A deal's a deal. I'll be collecting soon.

-C

The note in and of itself is enough to send me into a panic. But once it registers that the entire thing is written in blood, I'm hanging my head over the sink, violently expelling my pre-workout.

Come over. Now.

I hit send on the text before chucking my phone at the wall, not caring what damage is done. The fucker was *inside* my fucking apartment.

Less than five minutes go by before Roman is tearing through my front door, panic written all over his stubbled face. When he finds nothing amiss, a look of confusion flits over his handsome features before he makes his way to me.

I simply point at the note, refusing to touch it even long enough to hand it to him. Turning to stare out the windows of the living room, I wait. Wait for a reaction of any kind. Seconds go by. Five. Then ten. Thirty perhaps.

"Get your things," he says simply, slamming the note down on the island before stomping through the space, checking every nook and cranny, knowing he won't find anyone there. If they had been here, I wouldn't have stood a chance. I would be gone.

"What?!" I half-yell. "To go where? This is my home, Roman!" I whirl around to face him, fury pumping through my veins where the anxiety had lived mere moments ago.

"You can't stay here. We both know that," he says, stopping long enough to level me with a look. "Get your things," he says again, more emphatically than before. The voice that leaves him is unrecognizable, more beast than man now.

Knowing I don't have a leg to stand on in this fight, I do as I was told. He's right anyway. I can't stay here. They got in once. There's nothing stopping them from getting in any other time. My life hangs in the balance now.

He blows out a frustrated breath before rearing back and punching the wall in the kitchen, caving in the drywall around his hands. I watch as he pulls his hand away, knuckles starting to well with blood and vibrant red. Our eyes lock but not a word is said.

Turning on my heel, I head to the bedroom and start shoving anything I might need into an old bag. A few outfits, hairbrush, toothbrush, shampoo, the normal stuff.

An overwhelming dread and sadness drapes over me as I pack my life into the little bag, leaving my home and my normal life for who knows how long. Maybe forever.

The thought that I may have already lived my last normal day has my stomach churning again. The initial shock of that possibility wears off quickly though, as my blood turns to ice and everything goes numb inside me. A survival technique I learned a long time ago, during a period when things with Dawson were particularly bad. You can withstand just about anything if you can make yourself numb to it.

Exiting the bedroom, I do my best to shake the thought. It's all about forward motion now. Old life be damned.

"Ready?" he asks, face drawn and far away.

"As I'll ever be," I say honestly. This isn't something I ever considered facing in this lifetime or the next, but it's reality now. Time to get a game plan.

Roman pulls his phone from his pocket, dialing a number. "I need you to find out everything you can on Cain. Now," he says, pausing to let the other person speak. "No. This is top priority now. Everything else be damned."

He hangs up the call by dropping the phone to the floor and crushing it with the heel of his foot.

There's a fire burning in his eyes when he looks back at me, like the world is about to pay for Cain's threat. I've never been so absolutely terrified and turned on all at the same time.

Holding out his hand to me, we make our way out of the apartment and toward an unknown future. With a reassuring squeeze, we cross the threshold and I don't dare look back.

Chapter Twenty-Seven

Roman

"Finn, I need you here like yesterday," I say into the phone, my grip so tight my knuckles hurt. "No. It can't wait." Hanging up, I eye Jade, finding her in the same spot she's been in for the last hour.

We got new phones that can't be traced back to us, ditched anything that could, and headed back to my apartment for now until we can come up with a better plan. At the very least, she's not alone and my apartment would be a lot more difficult to break into than hers. Through the years, I've updated everything from the window locks to the doors themselves, including an insanely advanced security system.

Nobody is getting in here without me knowing about it and that simple fact makes me feel a fuck ton better about having her here. This is going to be the safest place for her right now.

"Hey," I say, sitting down beside her and pulling her into my side. "We've got this. Finn is on his way, and Sara is digging up anything valuable on the fucker right now. We're going to keep you safe and out of his grimy hands." Kissing the top of her head, I feel her relax slightly, likely just exhausted from the events of the day instead of actually believing a word that just came out of my mouth.

"I just need some time to sort through it all. It's way too much to process," she says, looking over at me through those gorgeous thick lashes. Her eyes are watery, but she manages to keep the tears at bay. "A month ago, I was a regular woman. With a pretty normal job. With a boyfriend and a house. I had a whole life planned out," she sighs, still reluctant to give up her past ambitions. "Now look at me." She drops her hands to her lap, dropping her chin right along with them.

I pull my arm back and turn her to face me. "We're not going to have any of that. No talking down on yourself, and damn sure no pity. It's a house rule," I say, putting the fingers of my right hand under her chin and lifting her face to look at me. "That's not the girl I know anyway. That girl isn't a quitter, and she sure as hell wouldn't want pity from anyone. She's a fighter."

She sniffles before nodding, pulling her chin from my fingers. As much as it goes against every nerve in my body, I let her. She's fighting a war I can't even see right now, and I have no desire to make that any harder for her.

A knock on the door interrupts our moment, and if I'm being entirely honest, I'm thankful for it. Awkward silences full of people feeling bad for themselves just aren't my cup of tea.

Looking through the peephole, I click back the lock and swing the door open for Finn. He looks to either side of him, making sure no one is around, before stepping through the doorway.

"Cain is coming for her," I say as he slips off his shoes in the entryway, not wanting to waste any time with pleasantries.

"I'm fine on this glorious day, Roman. Thank you for asking," he says sarcastically, even adding an eye roll for some extra drama.

When I turn to face him, the look he receives stops him in his tracks. "This is not a time for drama or games, Finn. If I wanted any of that, I would have called someone else."

"Point taken," he says, holding up his hands in mock surrender. "Tell me everything you know."

After telling him about the note, where it was found, and the things I currently know about in Cain's recent history, Finn leans back against the chair, fingers steepled in his lap.

"This is the guy you worked with before? Years ago?" he asks.

"Yeah. He's the one. I wanted to keep him on board because I knew he was capable of anything to get what he wanted and I didn't particularly want that released into the world without someone overseeing it," I say, pinching the bridge of my nose between my thumb and middle finger.

My phone buzzes on the coffee table with an incoming text. Opening the text thread, I find the new message. It's from Sara.

I'm on my way to see you.

Fuck. That can't be good.

"Looks like we will be having even more company soon," I say, placing the phone back on the table without a reply. "Sara's on her way."

Jade looks at me nervously, fidgeting with her sleeves again now. "That doesn't sound promising."

"No, it doesn't," I agree, not trying to sugarcoat anything for her. "But I can guarantee it's urgent."

We sit in a tense silence until there's a light knock on the door signaling Sara's arrival. I let her in and rejoin the others, grabbing a water for everyone on my way past the kitchen.

Placing her laptop on the coffee table, she kneels before it. Opening it, she types in her password before turning it face us. A video is paused on the screen. It's facing an open warehouse, nothing really jumping out as abnormal from the still screen. When she hits play, it's the audio that stands out.

Two men, standing off to the side but partially visible still, in a heated discussion. Both men keep their hands tucked neatly into the pockets of their dress pants but the conversation is animated nonetheless.

"You can't be fucking serious, Mack," the guy with the slicked back hair says. His hair is dark, and even from here, it looks like Dawn wouldn't remove all the grease from your hand if you touched it.

"I absolutely am serious," the bald guy, Mack, says, leaning against the wall, one foot crossed over the other ankle. "It's not my call and you know that."

"I don't give a fuck whose call it is! This is a death wish, and I don't know about you, but I've got some shit left to do before I go about signing my own death certificate," he says, pulling one hand from his pocket to run it through his grimy hair. "There's no way this will pan out. It won't go in our favor. You know that."

"Listen, Alec, it's out of my hands," Mack says, pulling his own hands from his pockets to lace his fingers together at his waist. "Boss's orders. What he says goes. Get a team together. It goes down tomorrow. We'll meet in the morning for the official details."

"You've gotta be kidding me," grimy hair, now known as Alec, says as he rubs his face to clear the look of terror that is clear even from the distance of the camera. "He's going to get us all killed! Roman will never let us leave that place alive!"

Sara shuts the laptop, tucking it back into the bag at her side before sitting back on her heels and looking between the three of us.

"I wasn't supposed to be able to get into their system. It took way longer than I expected, but it was worth it. Just crossing my fingers I covered my tracks and they can't tell I was in their files," she says, looking legitimately concerned now.

"I hate that we dragged you into this, Sara," I say, honestly meaning it. "I didn't have anyone else who could get me what I needed. This is a matter of life or death for Jade. Hell, for all of us now."

"What do we do now?" is her only response. No time for dwelling on the past or the reasons that landed her here alongside us. We're all in this together now, come what may.

"Now we need to make sure you can get onto that feed in the morning, first thing. Who knows how early they'll be meeting and we can't miss that. Find out anything else you can on Cain. I want to know everything about his last six months of operations. Who he uses, their technology, their weapons. I want to know every detail," I say as she nods in understanding. Her role is going to be vital to keeping Jade safe and here with me.

"Finn, I'm going to need your help here, of course. The apartment has some measures in place already, but not nearly enough to fend off Cain, especially if he's calling in the help of his guys." Finn nods, getting up from the chair to get started, looking around the apartment while making a list of what needs to be done and when.

"We are going to help Finn, but also prepare you as much as we can. This fight with Cain is going to be just as much mental as it is physical for you, love. I'm going to need your undivided attention. You've got to do everything I say, exactly as I say it. No hesitation." She nods, looking like a deer caught in headlights.

"The biggest thing you've got to remember is all is fair in love and war. He's going to be willing to do anything to get to you. Anything," I reiterate, holding her chin between my fingers so she looks at me directly. With the tiniest of nods, I drop my hand, hoping she truly understands but knowing she doesn't.

The entire evening is spent on apartment modifications and talks of plans for tomorrow. We even ordered Thai take-out so we didn't have to take a break, stuffing our mouths as we continued scurrying around the place. One day isn't nearly enough time, but it's all we have. I'm praying for a miracle at this point.

Hours later, we've done everything we can do. Adding longer screws to the door latches and hinges so they can't be kicked in nearly as easily. Double checking the locks on the windows. Updating the security system. Placing handguns with extra ammo where they'll be easy to get to when they're needed.

I sent Jade to bed when she wasn't able to hold her eyes open anymore, regardless of the attempt she was giving it. She's a trooper for sure. But being dead on her feet when they come won't be doing any of us any favors.

Restless, I tick through every tiny detail over and over again in my head, looking for anything that might give us an advantage. I'm still coming up empty. I trained the guy, but he's nothing like he was all those years ago. There was very little moral compass then, but that's gone now from what I've heard.

Scrubbing my hands through my hair hard enough I think it may pull some of it out by the roots, I release the pent-up frustration in a massive sigh as I push to my feet.

Pulling my shirt over my head, I turn the shower on to warm up as I step out of my pants and peel off my socks before tossing them into the basket in the corner.

Lathering and scrubbing my body, I beg my mind to quiet. I've got to get some rest if I'm going to be able to bring my A game tomorrow, and that's nonnegotiable.

I towel dry my hair and body before slipping on my boxers and sliding into bed behind her. Instantly, her warmth envelops me, reminding me that the world isn't always such a cold and miserable place. There's still happiness to be found here and there.

And that's worth dying for.

Chapter Twenty-Eight

Jade

Forcing my eyes to open against the bone-crushing exhaustion, I take in my surroundings. It takes a few seconds to remember I'm still in Roman's apartment instead of mine. The soft light filtering in past the curtains means it must still be fairly early.

Relaxing back against the mattress, I snuggle closer against him, relishing the feel of his skin against mine. I must have slept like a rock last night considering I don't even remember him coming to bed.

With building frustration, I give up on getting comfortable and falling back asleep. It's no use. Today is too important and I'm feeling anxious already. Cain's plans are set to go down today at some point. God only knows when that's going to happen and it's got me on edge.

Uncurling myself from his body, I slip out of bed without waking him. He's going to need all the rest he can get to get through today.

Quietly, I make my way to the kitchen to start a pot of coffee, doing my best to be as silent as a church mouse. Sara and Finn both ended up crashing here last night. We all decided it was for the best, just in case the attack came first thing this morning. Better to be safe than sorry.

Just as the coffee finishes brewing, Sara sits down at the island, laptop in front of her. She looks at me through sleepy eyes before ducking her head and getting to work. I place a cup of steaming coffee down beside her, which she receives with a tight smile.

With just a nod, I head for the living room, needing a few minutes to myself. My head is spinning with thoughts of everything that has happened over the last day or two and it's taking every ounce of willpower I've got to keep myself from coming apart at the seams. And that would be detrimental to everyone here, not just myself.

After scanning through the videos from last night, as well as dropping into the live feed in the warehouse, Sara closes her laptop, tiptoeing over to face me.

"I'm going to go home for a bit. Get a shower and some clothes. I'll reopen the feed when I get there just in case anything happens. I'm assuming whatever he's planning will be a little later in the day since nobody has been in the warehouse since late yesterday evening. It would take a while for everybody to get gathered up and set anything in motion."

Nodding my agreement, I stand and walk her to the door, closing and locking it behind her. Leaning my back against it, I take in the depth of the situation I've landed myself in.

Not me. Emily. Before the blood has time to begin boiling yet again, I push off the door, hellbent on being productive instead of living in the past any longer. Being pissed at a dead girl isn't going to save my life.

Finn is the next to rise as the aroma of bacon and biscuits floats through the air, no doubt interrupting his sleep.

His hair is a mess on top of his head, clothes wrinkled from sleep, but he couldn't seem to care less. The lazy smile that covers his face is nothing short of charming. It's no wonder people seem to connect with him so easily, myself included. But there's something simmering beneath that friendly surface. Something cold and deadly. In less than a second, the image passes, leaving me with the charming man in front of me, taking the coffee I've poured and offered to him, as well as the plate of breakfast.

"Thank you for everything, Finn," I say, wincing at how ridiculous and lackluster the words sound. He's done so much for a total stranger in such a short period of time. I don't have the words to truly convey how much it means to me.

"Not a problem, princess," he says, winking at me while taking a bite of bacon.

"I mean it. Nobody has ever done what you've done for me. Well, except Roman, obviously," I say with a small smile.

"Well god I would hope not! That would mean you've been in this god forsaken situation before and that would just be kind of fucked up," he says with a chuckle. "Seriously though," he says, taking on a more controlled tone now. "It's nothing he wouldn't have done for me. If you're important to him, you're important to me."

I nod, not sure what else to say as the moment hangs awkwardly between us. As if on cue, Roman shuffles into the kitchen, eyes bouncing between the two of us before raising an eyebrow.

Ducking out of the room to steal a moment to myself, I make my way back to the bathroom to freshen up and prepare for the day as best I can.

Turns out, there was nothing to prepare for. Literally nothing happened during the course of the day. Sara came back over in a couple hours, telling us how there had been no meeting at any point. In fact, the warehouse had remained entirely empty all morning.

There had been no texts or phone calls between Cain and any of his guys that would indicate anything was being planned or executed.

Literally. Nothing.

Sitting around waiting the entire day built my anxiety up to proportions I never considered possible. We talked. We played games. We strategized. We talked possibilities. None of it really helped to ease the feeling of my chest tightening until I couldn't breathe properly.

Something felt wrong.

"There's something we're missing," I said for the millionth time just to have it dismissed yet again.

"We aren't missing anything, Jade," Roman said patiently for the umpteenth time. "We've been through every detail. Over and over. We've watched the videos, checked the live feeds from all over the warehouse. We've gone through the texts and listened to the phone calls."

"Okay, but why would they call it off? After all that talk yesterday about having the meeting this morning and initiating the plan?" I question, heart racing inside my chest. "They wouldn't just abandon that plan."

"Sometimes things happen that take priority," Finn reassures, shrugging his shoulders nonchalantly. "It happens all the time in this world. Emergencies that are a lot bigger fish than taking care of a small time debt like this one."

"He's right," Roman agrees, relaxing back into the couch once more. "It could have been any number of things truthfully. The only thing I do know is it doesn't look like anything is happening today so everybody should go home and get some rest."

I stand along with Sara and Finn before Roman wraps his hand around my forearm. "Obviously not you," he says, urging me to sit back down with him.

Rolling my eyes, I pull my arm from his grip and walk the others to the front door. "We'll call later. Let us know if anything changes," I say as they step through the door.

Making my way back to him, I wrap my arms around my waist, feeling paranoid about the entire day. "I'm telling you something is off, Roman. There's something coming and we have no clue what it is," I plead, begging him to at least justify my feelings on this.

"We know what's coming, babe," he says, gluing his eyes to mine. There's sympathy and concern lingering in the look, as well as understanding. "This isn't my first time dealing with something like this, but I fully understand that it is your first time. Finn wasn't lying when he said this happens all the time. Plans fall through. They'll have their meeting, and when they do, we'll be listening. We'll be ready whenever they decide to take action."

Settling in beside him, I do my best to put my feelings to the side, burying them deep inside. I can't get past the feeling rolling in my gut, can't quite make myself relax, but I try for his sake.

Chapter Twenty-Nine

Roman

An eerie feeling overtakes me as I wake suddenly, arm still wrapped around Jade. We'd finally called it a day and crashed around midnight. After we sent Sara and Finn home, we spent the evening talking through everything that hadn't happened and possibilities going forward.

Rubbing my temple to ease the building tension, I run it all through my head again. None of it makes any sense. No matter how much I reassured her this was fairly normal, I couldn't get past the heaviness in my stomach every time I thought about it. She was right when she said something was off. I just don't know what that something is yet.

After tossing and turning for what feels like hours, I toss back the cover and swing my feet out of the bed. Staying in bed isn't doing me any good.

You up?

Hitting send on the text, I snag a bottle of beer from the fridge, hoping to ease the stress just a bit, but after the first pull, I find myself pouring it down the drain. Drinking isn't going to help anything in this situation. It's just going to make my thoughts less clear than they already are. I need to focus.

Turning on some low music, I set my mind to the task at hand, focusing all my attention on it now. I need to get a step ahead of him. Hell, at least even with him. I'd settle for that right now.

Yeah, what's up? Trouble sleeping?

As much as I hate to admit needing help, I really could use another set of eyes on this one.

You could say that. Care to lend a hand?

Less than a minute goes by before I get another text from Finn saying he's on his way. The next breath comes a bit easier with that knowledge. If anybody can help me crack this, it's going to be Finn.

"Let's get this figured out," he says as soon as I crack the door open, and in this moment, I am eternally grateful to have a guy like him on my side. Any time I've ever needed him, no matter the time or circumstance, he was there without hesitation. Though we started out as co-workers, we quickly became friends and then brothers.

Half smiling at the thought, I close the door behind him and follow him back to the couch. Notes are spread out haphazardly across the coffee table and couch cushions. More questions than answers truthfully. I don't even know where to start with this mess.

Puffing out his cheeks with a sigh, Finn takes in the state of the living room. When he left, the room was tidy and organized. Not a thing out of place. Now it resembles the aftermath of a tornado.

"Alright," he says, voice lacking any sense of enthusiasm but plenty of determination. "Let's get this figured out. Clue me in."

I feed him all the details we went over yesterday, along with any thought I've had about what actually happened. All the things we didn't tell Sara and Jade last night. Things we've learned over the years of being in this business. None of it helps a bit and only leaves us more confused.

"You've got to think like you. Not the current you though. The version of you that trained Cain. That's how we're going to figure this out before it's too late. Think about why James pushed him out. Why he doesn't work with us anymore. We've got to think about the things we wouldn't do in order to find out his next move," Finn says, eyes coming to life.

"I'll be damned," I say, a sly smile creeping across my face. "I think you're onto something there."

Leaning back in the chair, a cocky grin slides into place. "Lay it on me. Tell me what's running through your head now."

"I think he's going to hit us when we least expect it. Not with a lot of guys. That would draw too much attention to them. Somebody would see them and remember that. It'll only be a handful of guys at most. Probably a sharp shooter, somebody good at extraction. Of course, Cain will be there himself to oversee it, though he'll probably hang back in the shadows. A couple of his toughest guys physically." Rattling off the details I would have taught him helps. It feels right. I just can't pinpoint the *where*. And that's going to be the most important part.

"It won't be here. That would be too obvious. He'll know I've got this place ready for something like that to go down. It'll be somewhere we can't fortify," I say, swallowing past the lump in my throat. I have no doubts we could win and keep her safe if he attacked here, but he knows that too.

Resting my elbows on my thighs, chin resting on my hand now, I close my eyes and do my best to picture it. As much as I try, I'm coming up blank. Cain is phenomenal at what he does, mostly because he anticipates the other guy's moves, but also because he's willing to stoop lower than anybody I've met before. As fucked up as it is, that's the greatest asset to have in this lifestyle, even if it does earn you a hefty list of enemies hellbent on revenge.

The realization hits me right as it hits Finn. I'm not going to be able to take care of this by myself after all, even with his and Sara's help.

"I need James's help," I say, breaking the silence. One look at Finn confirms what I'd been hoping to avoid. He agrees entirely.

"I know it's not what you wanted to do," he starts. "I don't think you have any other option at this point though. We don't have the manpower to go up against Cain's guys, especially without having a clue when or where they're going to hit us."

Squeezing my hand into a fist against my thigh, I nod, knowing he's right. If I want to keep Jade safe, going to James is going to be my best bet. He said he wouldn't help us before, but that was before Cain was thrown into the mix.

Finn nods as I stand from the couch and go to wake Jade. Stopping in the doorway, I take note of how beautiful she really is. She looks so peaceful, like a dreamworld where everything is right and the biggest worry we'd have is what to make for dinner.

Sliding into bed behind her, I wrap my arms around her and pull her close. A soft moan leaves her lips, deflating me instantly. Waking her to deal with the monster chasing us is the hardest thing I've ever had to do. It kills me knowing I'm waking her and throwing her into a situation destined to make her sick with anxiety and worry.

"Jade," I say softly into her ear while smoothing her hair away from her face. "It's time to get up, baby. We've got to go."

She moans louder now, clearly unhappy with being woken up. Snuggling into the cover further, she's made her position clear. As much as I would love to surrender to her, it's a no go this time around.

"Come on, sweet girl. You can sleep on the way if you must, but we've got to get going now," I say, a little more persistent this time. Pulling my arm from underneath her body seems to do the trick. She's up and moving in less than a second, trying to reclaim my hold on her. Unfortunately for her, I'm a bit too quick for her sleep-addled brain and I'm up off the bed before she can grab my arm to keep me with her.

"I'll be waiting in the living room with Finn," I say, leaning down to kiss her forehead as she pouts up at me. "You're beautiful when you pout," I whisper before giving her a chaste kiss and turning on my heel.

She groans her disproval but gets up anyway. Within a couple minutes, she joins us in the living room with a yawn. Not quite awake, but present nonetheless.

"Good morning, darling," Finn says, smile full of sunshine even at this early hour. I'm pretty sure I see daggers flying from Jade's eyes as she glares at him. Thinking better of adding a body to her list, she settles for an eye roll instead, causing him to snicker before being silenced by another death glare.

"Let's get going before she decides to actually kill you," I suggest, nudging him with my elbow.

Finn throws an arm around her shoulders before giving her a small squeeze. "She wouldn't do that. She'd miss me too much," he teases. When she ignores him entirely, he lets go with a small pout, earning him a wicked smile from her.

Even though I laugh at their playfulness, dread starts to filter in, sinking like a lead weight in my stomach. I hate being completely out of options. I hate having to beg for help, even after being told no already. I swore a long time ago that I would never be in this shitty position again, but here we are.

Closing the door tightly behind us, I take off toward the Audi, the other two falling into step behind me. Not a word is spoken on the short walk to the car. There are no words to cover what's coming our way shortly, so we settle for silence instead.

The drive is over before I know it, and I honestly don't remember half of it. As soon as I pulled out onto the road, my brain went numb. Not a single thought ran through my head as I mindlessly drove the same path I'd taken a million times to James's warehouse.

Parking the car around the corner, I hold the door open for Jade as she steps out. Finn is beside me right after, hands clapped against my shoulder in a steadying grip. A grip that's supposed to reassure me that I'm doing the right thing, even though every atom in my body is screaming the opposite. With a tight smile, I step away from the car.

One knock on the heavy metal door goes unanswered. A look of concern flits across Finn's face before he wipes it clean for Jade's sake. Clearing my throat, I knock again. Same response.

Just as Finn and I are reaching for the guns we have at our waists, the lock slides back. The door creaks open a couple inches at best. Otto peaks out from behind it, opening it a bit further when he sees it's us.

"Get in here," he says, all but pushing us through the door before quickly shutting and bolting it again.

"What's going on?" I question, glancing around the building for anything out of place.

"Weird shit. I've been in this building damn near every day for the last four years. I've heard every sound this thing makes, but something has been different today," he explains, voice barely more than a whisper.

"I'm assuming you've told James," I say, just to be certain.

"I did. He didn't take me seriously about it though. He's in his office if you're needing to see him," he says, turning back toward the door when a strange bang comes from just outside it.

Knowing Otto is a little freaked out spikes my adrenaline higher than it was back at the apartment. That man never gets uncomfortable about anything. He's seen it all in the years he's worked for James.

Clearing the thought from my mind, I head for the stairs with Jade right behind me. Finn stops at the bottom of the staircase, waving us on without him. Cocking an eyebrow at him, I decide not to question it and climb the steps to the landing.

Knocking on James's door with a deep breath, I wait for his response with baited breath. When none comes, I knock again before trying the handle. It turns freely, allowing me to swing the door open.

I find the same dimly lit office inside, lamp still shining on the desk. Nothing seems out of the ordinary here either. His laptop is on the desk with papers laying haphazardly on top and around it.

Making my way to the desk, my heart stops. On top of the laptop, along with the other paperwork, is a bright orange sticky note with a scrawled mess written across it.

It's nice to see you again, Roman.

-C

Fuck.

A door slams somewhere on the main floor before people are shouting – several from the sounds of it. Two gunshots pop off as the yelling continues, more doors opening and shutting downstairs.

In a blind panic, both about Jade and about the men out there that I consider brothers, I bolt for the door, dragging her along behind me.

Fuck! I wasn't prepared for this to happen here! My thoughts race as I take the stairs two at a time, desperate to reach Finn and Otto, along with whoever else might be here.

"Go hide and so help me God, don't come out until I come find you. Don't come out for anyone," I say, hands on each side of her face as I stare into her terrified eyes as they fill with tears.

She nods quickly, terror unlike any I've seen before on her face, before turning and running toward the storage rooms under the staircase.

Good girl, I think, praising her silently for finding somewhere dark and out of the way while simultaneously praying it's enough. If they find her, even God won't be enough to save them.

I find Finn crouched down behind some old boxes that were used to ship and receive ammo. After a quick once over, I breathe a sigh of relief that the only blood coming from him is from his shoulder. A bullet must have grazed his upper arm but nothing too serious.

"Where's Otto?" I ask in his ear, crouching beside him now.

He nods to his left. Scanning the back wall, I find him quickly enough. It's hard to tell from this far away, but he seems to be doing okay. Standing and holding his own at least.

"I'm running low on ammo," Finn says, amusement coating his face as he looks at the empty crates in front of us. "I can't hold them off much longer, man. We've got to come up with a plan. Fast."

As quickly as it started, all the gunfire stops. The silence that rings through the warehouse is enough to cause my ears to ring. We look at each other quickly, confusion etching Finn's face just as a man I've never seen before appears behind him.

Pulling the knife from my boot, I push Finn to the floor before swinging the blade at the newcomer. I'm too far away, missing him entirely, but it was enough to keep him from stabbing Finn thankfully.

The guy is tall, probably my height or so, thin but toned, with dark short hair and a chiseled jawline. As he holds his hands up, knife still poised in his right one, a bone chilling smile morphs his face into something so sinister it instantly turns my blood to ice.

Finn's eyes widen a fraction, the first time I've ever seen him look truly scared. In that moment, my heart skips a beat before thundering painfully inside my chest. All adrenaline gone, it takes every ounce of courage I have to turn around and face whatever is lurking behind me now.

My stomach hits the ground and panic takes over entirely as my brain registers what I'm seeing across the empty warehouse.

Five feet or so in front of the metal staircase, my worst nightmare is becoming reality. Jade takes two steps, stopping when she's fully illuminated by the giant overhead light. She stands tall, doing her best to be brave, but I can see her legs shaking even from this distance. As Cain closes the space between them, I understand why.

With a wicked smile plastered across his face, he pulls her back against him before pulling the gun from behind her and placing it at her temple.

"How nice of you to finally venture out, Roman," he starts, voice dripping with venom. "I've been waiting a long time."

Stepping out from behind the crates, I take a step toward them but stop dead in my tracks when he presses the muzzle into her temple harder, making her squeal. A wave of nausea rolls over me, threatening to take over entirely.

"What do you want, Cain?" I ask, doing my best to keep my voice even as my world crashes around me. Glancing back at Finn, I see he's now in the same predicament as Jade, though the knife-wielding guy from earlier isn't being as gentle as Cain. *Fucking hell.*

"Ya know. I had full intentions of letting it go once I found out Emily was dead. Then I found out your precious little girlfriend was the one who did it, and that piqued my interest, but I wasn't going to act on it. She had no part in this," he says, pausing for several beats, as if time has stopped ticking altogether.

"Then I found out how important she was to you, Roman. That sealed her fate. After everything you put me through, it seemed fitting to take the only thing you've ever given a fuck about," he continues, relaxing his hold on her a bit as his eyes burn holes through my skull.

"Why here?" I ask, trying to buy myself as much time as possible to come up with a new plan. If I can keep him talking, I have a shot at fixing this once and for all.

"Of course it would be here. This is the place that ruined my life. It seems like a great place to ruin yours," he explains, shrugging lightly. "Besides, after I caught your buddy messing with the security cameras in *my* building, I figured the one you lovingly called home for so long would have to suffice."

Mind in overdrive, I don't trust myself to form a full sentence at this point. Her life hangs in the balance, each word from me bringing this closer to an end, one way or the other.

"Let her go and we can figure this out. I'll give you whatever it is you want, as long as you let her go. She's innocent in all of this. We don't take innocents, remember?"

I bargain, feeling as if the walls of the warehouse are closing in on me. Every second he has that gun pointed at her head feels like an eternity.

"Deal," he says easily, the sly grin returning. "Crawl to me. Then I'll let her go." As a show of good faith, he drops the gun to his side and waits patiently.

As every fiber of my being screams at me to not obey him, I drop to my knees. Moving one leg and arm at a time, I slowly start the trek to the middle of the warehouse. The shit eating grin on his face is enough to keep my eyes boring through his skull.

Once I reach his feet, he makes good on his word. Pushing hard enough on her lower back to make her stumble, he sets her free as tears roll down her face. When she reaches for me, he raises the gun slightly as a deterrent.

"It's okay, baby," I say, doing my best to soothe her. "Go to Finn. He'll take care of you." She nods almost imperceptibly before running to him, crashing into his arms as the sobs explode from her chest. The sound fractures my soul in a way that could never be repaired.

"On your feet," he says, tapping my shoulder with the barrel of his gun. "Time to make amends."

Following his orders, I stand shakily. Not from fear now, but from the rage boiling in my veins from the pain this has caused Jade. She should've never been brought into this in the first place.

Chapter Thirty

Jade

Watching Roman climb to his feet in front of Cain has me coming undone inside, though I do everything in my power to keep it together on the outside. I know showing what I'm feeling would only make the situation worse for him, so I summon every drop of willpower I have left to hold myself together.

"The things you did to me here were unimaginable," Cain starts, speaking loud enough that his voice echoes through the mostly empty warehouse. "You beat me bloody, taught me the places that hurt the most on the body as well as the soul, and showed me there are no real morals in this

world. Except for keeping the innocents out of it, of course,"
he says, winking at me. It's enough to turn my stomach, even
from that distance.

"Then you threw me out on the street when I wasn't of
enough use to you anymore," he says, voice vibrating with
years of anger. "You tossed me out like trash, not caring where
I went. Not caring if I lived or died." The venom in his voice
has me trembling now. His face is contorted with barely
contained rage as he recalls the harsh times after he was
kicked out of here.

"I was only 17," he says, eyes drilling into Roman's. I
can see the hate that fills them from here. I can only imagine
how menacing they look that close. A shiver runs through me
at the thought. "I was just a kid."

"I could say I'm sorry, and I really am, but that's not
going to fix anything that happened, Cain," Roman says, voice
miraculously strong even in the face of what I'd consider pure
evil. "You went off the rails after I started teaching you. James
demanded that I let you go. You were reckless and that wasn't
a risk he was willing to take with the brand he'd built from the
ground up."

"I can't disagree there," Cain says, surprising us all. "I
did go off the rails a bit. Do you have any idea why that might
have been? What have you kept hidden from everybody all
these years, Roman?"

Hanging his head now, Roman takes his time before
speaking again. Raising his eyes to Cain's, he takes a deep

breath before admitting things I would've never seen coming from him.

"I can imagine it was because I fucked your girlfriend behind your back," he starts, confidence oozing from his voice now. "Or maybe it's because she wanted to leave you after she got railed by a real man. Or maybe it's the fact that I caught her beating an innocent kid damn near to death because he stole $4 from her purse while she wasn't paying attention, so I shot her in the head. It really could be any number of things."

Cain is shaking with fury by the time Roman finishes. It's a miracle he hasn't exploded from the way he's shaking.

"I fucking *loved* her, and you knew it!" he screams, pain echoing from every corner of the building. "You took her from me, and then you fucking killed her!"

"You're right," Roman agrees, stretching his arms out wide to either side of him. "There's nothing I can do but apologize at this point. I'll apologize for fucking her behind your back, but I won't apologize for killing her. That kid didn't deserve that. He was only six, Cain. He stole what he could to feed himself because his mom was too fucked up on drugs that *you* sold to her to even care if he ate or not. I'm not sorry for that." Holding his head high, Roman faces down the rawest form of evil I've ever encountered.

With every word, my chest tightens until it's painful to draw a breath.

"Maybe that's true, but maybe it's all another one of your lies to get what you want," Cain says, shaking the gun at Roman now. "I don't have the heart to kill her and take that from you. She doesn't deserve that. But in all honestly, she doesn't deserve this either," he says as he aims and pulls the trigger.

It feels like an eternity before the sound of the shot rings through the space around us. It feels even longer as I watch the blood spray from Roman's back, coating the floor behind him as he falls to his knees.

As a scream rips from my lungs, I run to him, though every step feels like it's in slow motion. It takes too long to reach him, too long to pull him into my arms as I watch Cain turn on his heel and run, just as gunshots ring out again. The sound comes from behind me this time. Finn fires his pistol at Cain and his guys as they make their way toward their one shot at freedom.

Cain cries out as a bullet hits home, piercing his calf. Blood runs down his leg as he hobbles to the door and then out into the world beyond it. As the door slowly closes, the dimness of the warehouse filters back in, along with the silence.

Pulling him into my lap, his blood covers my legs and hands, warm and slick. Sobs rip from my soul as I watch the only man I've ever truly loved bleed out in my lap, helpless to change the circumstances.

As he swallows against the pain, he gives me that shit-eating grin I've fallen in love with over time. A single tear slips down his cheek, mixing with the blood now covering everything beneath us.

"I'll find you in the next one," he says breathily. "And I'll be loving you until then, baby." Slowly, he uses what energy he has left to raise his hand and cover mine, giving it a reassuring squeeze as everything crashes around us.

"God, I fucking love you, Roman. I'll make him pay for this. I swear it," I sob, leaning down to kiss his lips as he pulls a final breath into his lungs. With that exhale, he's gone.

Cradling his head against my chest, I rock back and forth for only God knows how long. Finn doesn't interrupt until my sobs have subsided. The tears are still there, but my lungs are raw, making it impossible for a sound to leave my lips now.

"We have to go now," he says gently, eyes full of misery and pain. "He's gone, Jade."

Kissing his sweet lips one final time, I gently lower his eyelids, praying he finds rest while he waits for me on the other side.

"I'm coming, baby," I whisper to him before laying him onto the floor as gently as possible. "I've got a loose end to tie up first, then I'm coming to you."

Standing with Finn's help, I take one last look at Roman. Chest on fire, I nod slowly to Finn, letting him lead me to the back door and out into a new world. A world without Roman.

With sirens in the background, we break into a steady run, needing to get as far from the warehouse as possible, especially seeing as I'm covered in fresh blood.

"So, what now?" I ask, fire burning in my veins. As the old saying goes, hell hath no fury like a woman scorned.

9 7 9 8 9 9 0 1 7 4 2 0 7